"Look," Clint said, "what was this all about? I'd like to know why I ended up killing men I didn't know."

Bodie shoved his chair back.

"We can talk about that later," he said. "I've got somethin' I've got to do."

He stood up and started away.

"Now, wait a minute," Clint said, chasing after him. They got outside before Bodie stopped and turned to face him.

"I need to know what's going on," Clint said.

"What's going on is you poked your nose in somebody else's business," Bodie said.

"It's always my business when somebody's outnumbered," Clint said.

"Look, I've got things to do, Adams," Bodie said. "I'll see you later about all this."

"Yeah, okay," Clint said. "We'll talk later. But know this . . . I'm not leaving town until I know what the hell this is all about."

DON'T MISS THESE
ALL-ACTION WESTERN SERIES
FROM THE BERKLEY PUBLISHING GROUP

THE GUNSMITH by J. R. Roberts
Clint Adams was a legend among lawmen, outlaws, and ladies. They called him . . . the Gunsmith.

LONGARM by Tabor Evans
The popular long-running series about Deputy U.S. Marshal Custis Long—his life, his loves, his fight for justice.

SLOCUM by Jake Logan
Today's longest-running action Western. John Slocum rides a deadly trail of hot blood and cold steel.

BUSHWHACKERS by B. J. Lanagan
An action-packed series by the creators of Longarm! The rousing adventures of the most brutal gang of cutthroats ever assembled—Quantrill's Raiders.

DIAMONDBACK by Guy Brewer
Dex Yancey is Diamondback, a Southern gentleman turned con man when his brother cheats him out of the family fortune. Ladies love him. Gamblers hate him. But nobody pulls one over on Dex . . .

WILDGUN by Jack Hanson
The blazing adventures of mountain man Will Barlow—from the creators of Longarm!

TEXAS TRACKER by Tom Calhoun
J.T. Law: the most relentless—and dangerous—manhunter in all Texas. Where sheriffs and posses fail, he's the best man to bring in the most vicious outlaws—for a price.

THE GUNSMITH

375

THE THOUSAND-MILE CHASE

J. R. ROBERTS

JOVE BOOKS, NEW YORK

THE BERKLEY PUBLISHING GROUP
Published by the Penguin Group
Penguin Group (USA) Inc.
375 Hudson Street, New York, New York 10014, USA

Penguin Group (Canada), 90 Eglinton Avenue East, Suite 700, Toronto, Ontario M4P 2Y3, Canada (a division of Pearson Penguin Canada Inc.) • Penguin Books Ltd., 80 Strand, London WC2R 0RL, England • Penguin Group Ireland, 25 St. Stephen's Green, Dublin 2, Ireland (a division of Penguin Books Ltd.) • Penguin Group (Australia), 707 Collins Street, Melbourne, Victoria 3008, Australia (a division of Pearson Australia Group Pty. Ltd.) • Penguin Books India Pvt. Ltd., 11 Community Centre, Panchsheel Park, New Delhi—110 017, India • Penguin Group (NZ), 67 Apollo Drive, Rosedale, Auckland 0632, New Zealand (a division of Pearson New Zealand Ltd.) • Penguin Books (South Africa) (Pty.) Ltd., Rosebank Office Park, 181 Jan Smuts Avenue, Parktown North 2193, South Africa • Penguin China, B7 Jiaming Center, 27 East Third Ring Road North, Chaoyang District, Beijing 100020, China

Penguin Books Ltd., Registered Offices: 80 Strand, London WC2R 0RL, England

This is a work of fiction. Names, characters, places, and incidents either are the product of the author's imagination or are used fictitiously, and any resemblance to actual persons, living or dead, business establishments, events, or locales is entirely coincidental.

THE THOUSAND-MILE CHASE

A Jove Book / published by arrangement with the author

PUBLISHING HISTORY
Jove edition / March 2013

Copyright © 2013 by Robert J. Randisi.
Cover illustration by Sergio Giovine.

ISBN: 978-0-515-15316-3

JOVE®
Jove Books are published by The Berkley Publishing Group, a division of Penguin Group (USA) Inc., 375 Hudson Street, New York, New York 10014. JOVE® is a registered trademark of Penguin Group (USA) Inc. The "J" design is a trademark of Penguin Group (USA) Inc.

PRINTED IN THE UNITED STATES OF AMERICA

10 9 8 7 6 5 4 3 2 1

ALWAYS LEARNING   **PEARSON**

ONE

Clint Adams was attracted by the shots.

Now, many men probably would have heard them and ridden the other way. Sometimes Clint wished he were that kind of man. It would have saved him a lot of trouble over the years.

But since he wasn't that kind of man, he rode in the direction of the shots. He came to the top of a rise and reined in. Below him was one man, who had taken cover behind a felled tree, being fired upon by six others. Even though he didn't know who they were—lawmen, outlaws, whatever—it seemed kind of one-sided to him.

With these kinds of odds, he just naturally went with the low man.

The man behind the fallen tree was firing with a rifle, but pretty soon he'd have to go to his pistol, if he had one. Clint could see that the six men firing at him—from behind trees, in dry washes, or just plain flat on their bellies—had rifles and handguns. Farther behind them—just below where Clint was sitting astride Eclipse—were their horses, tied to some bushes.

Clint dismounted, backed Eclipse out of sight, then made his way carefully down the hill to the horses. Quickly, while the firing was still going on, he went through their saddlebags. He found nothing to indicate that they might be lawmen of any kind—sheriff's deputies, deputy marshals, or even Arizona Rangers.

He wondered if he could get the man out of this predicament without killing anyone.

Tom Angel wondered who the six men were, and why they were shooting at him. They couldn't be who he was thinking about, or he was in real trouble. Not that this wasn't already plenty of trouble. He also wondered who the man behind them was, the one who had come down the hill to their horses. They didn't see him, but Tom did.

Angel had been riding along on his way to Tucson when the six men suddenly appeared, riding hell-bent for leather toward him, firing their weapons. His horse went down, and he was forced to take cover behind this fallen tree, which had turned out to be very good cover. The animal got up and ran off, so maybe when this was over—and he was still alive—he'd be able to run it down.

But for now, he was concerned with the keeping alive part . . .

Clint untied all the horses and tried to quietly shoo them along. He had some help when, just at that moment, there was a barrage of shots that spooked the animals. They ran off, and Clint took cover behind the bushes.

One of the six men turned, saw what was happening, and shouted, "Hey, the horses!"

"What?" another man said, turning also. "The horses!"

All the men turned.

"Get them!" one of them yelled.

"What about Angel?"

"He's on foot," the man said. "We'll be able to catch up to him again if we aren't on foot, too. Now come on!"

He was an older man, who must have been the leader. He started running after the horses while some of the younger men outpaced him.

While the men ran after their horses, Clint went back up the hill to Eclipse and mounted up. After making sure the men were still chasing their horses, he rode over to where the man they called Angel was still crouched behind a dead tree.

Tom Angel watched as the man rode toward him on his horse. Warily he stood up, not knowing who this feller was or what he wanted. What he did know was that the man had helped him. He held his rifle loosely, but ready . . .

"Where's your horse?" Clint asked as he reached the man.

"He went down when they started shooting, but he got up and ran off. Might be lame for all I know."

Clint looked behind him, then back at the man, reaching his hand out.

"You better hop on before they come back. Let's see if we can run your horse down."

"Appreciate it," the man said.

He grabbed Clint's arm and leaped up onto Eclipse behind Clint.

"Helluva a horse you got here," he said.

"Yeah, he'll carry the two of us until we can find yours. But we better get the hell out of here before your friends get back."

"No friends of mine," Angel said.

"That was the impression I got."

TWO

They put some distance between themselves and the six men and found Angel's horse, a sorrel, standing and grazing. Clint stopped some distance away so as not to spook the animal and let Angel approach it on foot. He watched as the man spoke to the animal, then patted his neck, finally leaned over to check his legs. He then walked back to where Clint was still sitting astride Eclipse.

"He's got a skinned knee, but that's about it," Angel said. "He should be okay. I'll have him looked at when we get to town."

"What town?" Clint asked.

Angel shrugged and said, "I don't know."

"Where were you headed?"

"Nowhere in particular."

"And those six, they just jumped you?"

"Yeah," Angel said, "came out of nowhere."

"And you don't know them."

"Nope."

"Or why they attacked you."

"Nope."

"You got a price on your head?"

"Not that I know of."

"What's your name?" Clint asked. "I heard one of them call you Angel."

"Tom," the man said, "Tom Angel."

Clint shook his head.

"Don't know the name."

"And what's yours?" Angel asked. "Who do I have to thank for saving my bacon back there?"

"Clint Adams."

Angel froze and stared at Clint.

"You're kiddin'."

"No, I'm not."

"The Gunsmith?"

"That's right."

"Why would you stop to help me?"

"I have a habit of sticking my nose in other people's business," Clint said.

"Well," Angel said, "I'm pretty glad you did. Where are you headed?"

"I thought I'd stop in Tucson and see how things are going."

"Sounds good to me," Angel said. "Mind if I ride along? Of course, you know if those six catch up to us . . ."

"Let's cross that bridge when we come to it," Clint said. "Tucson's the closest town, and you need somebody to look at your horse's leg. Get mounted."

Angel climbed aboard his horse, walked it around a few feet to test out the leg.

"Seems okay," Angel said, "but if we have to move fast, I'll never keep up with that beast of yours."

"Then let's hope we won't have to move fast," Clint said. "Let's get along."

* * *

They arrived in Tucson without encountering the six gunmen again.

"Who did you think they were?" Clint asked as they rode into town. "Lawmen?"

"No reason for lawmen to be after me," Angel said, "unless it was a mistake."

"Outlaws, then."

"Same difference," Angel said. "Why would a bunch of outlaws be after me? I can't figure it."

"Would you have any reason not to want to go to the sheriff here and tell him about it?"

"Nope," Angel said, "no reason. I thought I'd see to my horse, and then go and do that."

"Well," Clint said, "let me know if you need a witness." He pointed as they passed a saloon called the Ace High. "I'll be in that saloon after I get a hotel room."

"I'll see you there for a drink, no matter what," Angel said. "I owe you one—at least."

They rode to the livery stable together, arranged for the care of their horses, then walked back to the center of town with their saddlebags and rifles.

"I'm heading for a hotel," Clint said.

"I'm gonna get over to the sheriff's office, just in case those six jaspers ride into town."

"Good luck," Clint said. "Like I said, let me know if you need me to back your story."

"Thanks for all your help, Clint," Angel said. "I'll let you know what happens with Johnny Law."

Clint gave Angel a salute and the two men went their separate ways.

THREE

Clint went into the Hotel Congress, on Congress Street, and got himself a room. When he checked to make sure there was no easy access to his room by the window, he poured some water from the pitcher on the dresser into the basin, removed his shirt, and cleaned himself up as best he could.

He thought about helping Angel get away from the six men who were—apparently—trying to kill him. Usually, sticking his nose in other people's business got him into trouble. This time, however, he had managed to do it without being seen. As far as the six men knew, their horses had somehow gotten loose and run off. So maybe this time, things had turned out okay.

He dried himself off and donned a fresh shirt he took from his saddlebags, then left the room to head to the Ace High Saloon. Now that he'd cleaned the trail dust from the outer man, it was time to clean it from the inner man with a big, cold beer.

While Clint was in the hotel, Tom Angel approached the front door of the sheriff's office. He was not a man who spent a lot of time in the company of lawmen. While he had told Clint the truth that there was no paper out on him, he was not exactly the most law-abiding citizen. However, this was his first time in Arizona, and he couldn't see any reason not to talk to the sheriff. If those six men showed up in Tucson, he was going to have to defend himself, and he might as well make the local sheriff aware of the situation.

He went to the door, knocked, and entered. The man inside was sweeping the floor with a worn broom, looked up as Angel entered. He had the heavily lined face of a man who had seen a lot of life.

"Help you?" he asked.

"You the sheriff?"

"That's right. Sheriff Hastings. You got the look of a man who just rode into town."

"You know everybody in town that well, that you know I'm a stranger?" Angel asked.

"Pretty much," Hastings said. "Besides, you knocked. Nobody in this town knocks." He set the broom aside, and walked over to his desk. It was then Angel saw the badge on his chest.

"What can I do for you, friend?"

"I had a problem outside of town with some men."

"Some men?" the sheriff asked. "How many is some?"

"Six."

"What kind of problem?"

"They tried to kill me."

"Why?"

"I don't know."

"You sure they were tryin' to kill you?"

"Well, they were shootin' at me."

"You know who they were?"

"No idea."

"Why would they want to kill you?" the lawman asked again.

"Again, no idea."

The sheriff studied Angel critically.

"Any warrants out on you, friend?"

"No."

The lawman fell silent again.

"Look," Angel said, "I'm just tellin' you what happened. I ain't askin' you to go out there and look for them."

"What are you askin' me to do, then?"

"Not throw my ass in jail if they come to town and I have to defend myself."

"Uh-huh," Hastings said. "Well, I guess I can do that much."

"Fine."

Angel turned and walked to the door. The sheriff spoke before he could go out.

"You stayin' in town?"

"Yep."

"Where?"

"Don't know yet," Angel said. "Got any suggestions?"

Instead of answering, the sheriff asked, "How long you plan on stayin'?"

"I don't know."

"You got business here?"

"My horse was injured when those boys tried to kill me. I'm here to get him treated. When he can travel, I'll leave."

"Just try to stay out of trouble while you're here," the sheriff suggested.

"I can do that," Angel said, "if I'm left alone."

"I'm just askin' you to watch yerself, that's all," the lawman said.

Angel opened the door and before he went out said, "I guess I can do that."

FOUR

Clint entered the Ace High. At this time of the afternoon it was not busy. He went to the bar and the bartender approached him, asking, "What can I get ya?"

"Cold beer."

"Comin' up."

Clint looked around. There were about half a dozen men in the place and none of them were paying any attention to him.

"There ya go," the bartender said, setting a cold one in front of him.

"Thanks."

Clint picked it up and drank half of it down. The inner man immediately felt a lot better. He nursed the rest and then ordered a second. While he was drinking that one, Tom Angel walked in.

"Bring my friend a beer," Clint said to the bartender.

"I'm buyin, remember?" Angel said.

"Next one," Clint said.

Angel drank half of his down, heaved a large sigh.

"How'd it go with the sheriff?"

"Not sure he believed me," Angel said.

"I can talk to him if you like."

"He didn't exactly call me a liar," Angel said. "He just couldn't wrap his head around why six men would try to kill me if I wasn't wanted for something. I'm sure he's going through his posters now."

"Well, he won't find anything, right?"

"Right."

"So there's nothing to worry about."

"Unless those six show up here, lookin' for me."

"Which could happen," Clint said, "this being the closest town."

Angel finished his beer, put the empty mug down, noticed that Clint's was empty as well.

"Bring us another," he called to the bartender. "Let me buy you this one, and then I'll go and check on my horse."

"You looking to ride out if he's fine?"

"I dunno," Angel said with a shrug. "Might be stupid of me to wait here for those six to arrive. Movin' on might be the right thing to do."

"Sounds right to me," Clint said.

"Yeah," Angel said as the bartender put down two more beers.

A few miles outside of town, six men gathered in a field, five of them looking to their boss, Big Ed Callahan.

"Ed, what do we do?" one of them asked.

"He ain't anyplace," another said.

Callahan's number one man, Kenny Hunt, looked at him and said, "I don't like that all those horses got loose at the same time, Ed."

"I know," Callahan said, "he must've had help. Somebody snuck up behind us and let them horses go."

"So what do we do?" the first man asked. "Keep lookin'?"

Callahan gazed off into the distance.

"Tucson's over that way," he said.

"Closest town," Hunt said, agreeing.

"Okay," Callahan said, "then we'll go there. Maybe he needs a doctor."

"His horse went down," Hunt said, "then got up and ran off."

"So maybe the horse needs treatment," Callahan said. "Either way he'd go to Tucson."

"Kinda obvious," Hunt said.

"Whataya mean?" Callahan asked.

"I mean it's the closest town, so maybe he'll skip it."

"If he's hurt, or his horse is, he'll need treatment quick," Callahan said. "He's gotta go to Tucson."

"Okay," Hunt said, "so we go to Tucson."

"Good," one of the men said. "I could use a drink."

"You'll get your drink," Callahan said, "when I say so. Not before."

"Sure, boss."

The men looked at Hunt, who just shook his head at them then followed his boss.

"It's not too bad," the liveryman told Angel. "I put some poultice on it and wrapped it up. I'd say give him a couple of days."

"A couple of days?"

"Unless you wanna take a chance on him hurtin' himself by favorin' it."

"Yeah, I get it," Angel said. "Okay. Take good care of 'im."

"Yes, sir."

Angel left the livery. It looked like he was definitely going to need a hotel room. This wouldn't make the sheriff very happy, but then he wasn't exactly excited about it either.

FIVE

Clint was still in the Ace High Saloon when Tom Angel reappeared.

"You don't look like you got good news," he said as the man joined him at the bar.

"I didn't," Angel said. "Man says my horse needs a coupla days."

"So you're stuck here, unless you want to sell your horse and buy a new one."

"I'm kinda partial to that sorrel," Angel said. "I'd like to keep 'im."

"Well," Clint said, "maybe those six won't come to Tucson."

"I guess that depends on how smart they are," Angel said. "And I didn't get to know them long enough to tell."

"No, neither did I."

"I think I could use another beer," Angel said, waving to the bartender, "and a whiskey. You?"

"I'm good," Clint said, looking down at his half-filled mug of beer. It was his third, and he hadn't planned on having any more.

"Yeah, well," Angel said, accepting his drinks from the bartender, "these will be my last, too. You want to get somethin' to eat after this?"

"Sounds good," Clint said. "I could use a steak."

The six men came riding into Tucson, raking the street and boardwalks with their eyes, looking for Tom Angel.

"If he's here," Callahan said, "he's gonna be in a saloon, the whorehouse, or a café."

"Or a hotel," Hunt said.

"Maybe he went to the sheriff," one of the other men said.

"Naw, he wouldn't do that," Callahan said.

The others didn't comment because their boss knew Angel the best.

"Okay, look," Callahan said, "we're gonna split up into twos. If you see him, don't brace him. Come and find me. We're gonna take him together. Understand?"

"Yeah, we understand," Hunt said.

"Kenny, take Tino with you," Callahan said. "Lumpy, you're with me. Joe, you and Vinnie stay together—and keep him out of trouble."

"I don't start trouble," Vinnie said.

"First time you see a pretty girl, you're lookin' for trouble," Callahan said. "If you cause trouble this time because of a girl, I'll shoot you myself. You got it?"

"I got it, boss."

"Okay. Split up here. I don't want all the horses in the same place. It'll be too noticeable."

They broke off into their three groups. Callahan and Lumpy rode past the sheriff's office, but Callahan hardly gave it a look.

Hunt and Kenny rode past the bank and the hardware store, then came to the mercantile.

"Let's dismount here," Hunt said. "We'll check inside the store, and then go on foot."

Joe and Vinnie rode past a few stores and then came to a saloon.

"Let's get a drink," Vinnie said.

"You heard what the boss said," Joe responded.

"Come on, one drink," Vinnie said. "I'm parched. I'm not gonna cause no trouble. Come on."

"Vinnie—" Joe started, but the man had already turned his horse toward the saloon. Joe hurried after him. They both stopped in front of the saloon and dismounted.

"One beer," Joe said as they went into the Ace High Saloon. "Just one."

"Don't worry," Vinnie said.

"I'm not," Joe said. "You're the one the boss said he was gonna shoot."

Clint and Angel walked a few blocks, then came to a small café that had STEAKS AND CHOPS stenciled on the front window.

"This is the place," Angel said.

"Fine with me. Let's go."

They went inside and were seated near the back of the small room. Only a couple of the other tables were occupied, and those people were paying attention to their food.

"We're beatin' the crowd," Angel said.

The waiter came over and Clint ordered a steak with everything.

"I'll have the same," Angel said.

"With everything?" the waiter asked.

"Everything that I can get."

"Right away."

"And a pot of coffee," Clint said.

"Yes, sir."

"I could eat my horse right now," Angel said.

"If you did that, you'd be able to buy another one, and then leave."

"Ha, ha," Angel said.

Joe and Vinnie had a beer in the Ace High and then Joe practically dragged the other man out of the saloon.

"Come on," Vinnie complained, "one more—"

"No, that's it!" Joe said outside. "I ain't gettin' shot by the boss because of you. Let's walk and look."

"Fine, walk," Vinnie said. "Maybe we'll come to another saloon."

"No saloons, Vinnie!"

Clint and Angel were working on their steaks when Angel looked out the window and saw two men going by.

"Oh, great," he said.

"I've had better," Clint said. "This is kind of tough—"

"No, outside," Angel said. "Out the window."

"What?"

"Two of the men who were shootin' at me just went by."

Clint put down his knife and fork and looked out the window. He didn't see anybody.

"Are you sure?"

"I recognized them," Angel said.

"Did they look in and see you?"

"I don't think so."

"Well," Clint said, "if they're here, the others must be here, too."

"So what do I do now?" Angel asked.

"Finish your steak," Clint said, "and I'll finish mine." Clint picked up his knife and fork. "If they didn't see you, this is the best place for you right now."

SIX

"Did you see him?" Joe asked.

"See who?"

"The guy. Angel."

"Where?"

"Back there, as we passed that café. I looked in the window and saw him."

"What was he doin'?"

"He's in a restaurant," Joe said. "Whataya think he's doin'? He's eatin'."

"I'm kinda hungry myself," Vinnie said. "If he's in there, let's go in and eat."

"And let him see us?"

"What's he gonna do?" Vinnie asked. "We're in a restaurant."

"Yeah, well, he wasn't alone."

"Who was he with?"

"I don't know," Joe said impatiently. "Look, the boss said if we saw him, not to go near him."

"We ain't gonna go near him," Vinnie said. "We're just gonna get us a steak."

"No, we ain't," Joe said. "We're gonna go find the boss."

"Ah, geez," Vinnie said, following Joe. "I didn't even see 'im . . ."

Callahan and Lumpy had checked two saloons and three restaurants without finding Tom Angel.

"Let's check some hotels," Callahan said.

"Why don't we split up, boss?"

"No, we stay together," Callahan said. "I don't want anybody bein' caught alone by Angel."

They were about to cross the street when they saw Joe and Vinnie running toward them.

"We found 'im, boss," Joe said, out of breath.

"Where?"

"He's at a steak and chop house a few streets over." Joe looked behind him. "I think it's a few streets. We been runnin' . . ."

"I didn't see him," Vinnie said.

"That don't surprise me, Vinnie," Callahan said. "Okay, let's find Kenny and Tino and then we'll take him."

"What about the law?" Lumpy asked.

"Don't worry about the law," Callahan said. "We're gonna do what we came here to do. I'll deal with the law later. Come on."

Clint and Angel finished their steaks, followed them with pie and coffee. Angel kept looking out the window.

"Relax," Clint said. "They won't come in here."

"What makes you say that?"

"There's no room in here," Clint said. "They'd be in each other's way. No, they'll wait for you to come out."

"Maybe I should go out the back."

"They'll have the back covered."

"Yeah, but most of them will be in the front," Angel said. "I'll have a better chance in the back."

"Finish your pie and coffee," Clint said, "and then I'll go out the front and see what's going on."

"Why?" Angel asked. "I mean, why would you risk your life like that?"

"Well," Clint said, "it's my fault you're in this mess."

"How do you figure that?"

"Without me," Clint said, "they would've killed you out there in that field."

SEVEN

Clint and Angel walked to the front of the café and looked out the window. Between the words STEAK and CHOPS, they saw six men standing across the street.

"They're all out front," Angel said. "Come on, we can go out the back."

"We could," Clint said, "but then they'll keep chasing you. And how far are you going to get without your horse?"

"Okay, so I'll sell the horse and buy another one."

"You don't strike me as the type of man who wants to be on the run, Tom."

"Who wants to be on the run, Clint?" Angel asked. "But what choice do I have? I can't stand against six men. I'm not you."

"I wouldn't want to face six men either," Clint said, "but maybe neither of us will have to."

"What do you mean?"

"I'll go out and talk to them," Clint said. "Maybe I can convince them to give up."

"Why would you do that?"

"Maybe I can keep somebody from getting killed," Clint said. "Wait here, and watch."

"I'll watch your back," Angel said. "If any of them makes a move for his gun, I'm comin' out."

"Okay, Tom," Clint said. "That sounds good."

"Who's the guy in there with him?" Callahan asked Joe and Vinnie.

"I didn't see nothin'," Vinnie said.

"I saw them," Joe said, "but I don't know who the other fella is."

"Well," Callahan said, "he must be some friend or partner of Angel's. That means he dies, too, if he gets in the way."

"Hey, boss," Lumpy said.

They all looked across the street, saw a man step out of the café.

"That him?" Callahan asked. "That the other fella?"

"That's him," Joe said.

"Well, here he comes . . ."

Clint stepped into the street and started across. He didn't know if he was doing the right thing. Maybe he should have let Angel go out the back door and run. Tom Angel wasn't the Gunsmith. Clint would never be able to use the back door, because then word would get around and he'd be an even bigger target than he already was. But Angel couldn't keep running. Nobody could.

"Nobody move unless I do," Callahan said to his men. "Get it?"

Nobody answered until Hunt said, "We got it."

"Gentlemen," Clint said, stopping in front of the men. Not too close, just enough room to move if he had to.

"The name's Callahan," the older man said. "They call me Big Ed."

"Is that a fact?" Clint asked. "And why do they do that?" Clint didn't find the man to be particularly big.

"What's your name, friend, and why are you poking your nose in my business?"

"My name is Clint Adams," Clint said.

Callahan stared at him, then a look of doubt appeared on his face.

"You're lyin'."

"Why would I do that?"

"So I won't kill you and your friend."

"Why do you want to kill my friend?"

"He hasn't told you?"

"No."

"Well," Callahan said, "that's his business. Maybe I'll give him time to tell you before you both die."

"I'm thinking nobody has to die."

"And why's that?"

"You and your boys can just ride out."

"Let's say you are who you say you are," Callahan replied. "Why would you stand with him?"

Clint looked at all six men, then said, "I hate six-to-one odds. It's just not fair."

"I'll tell you what," Callahan said. "I'll give you the same chance. Mount up and ride out. Leave him to me."

"I can't do that."

"Then go back and talk to him," Callahan said. "Maybe he'll save your life by comin' out by himself. Either way, I'll be waitin'."

"I can't talk you out of this?" Clint asked.

"Even if you are the Gunsmith," Callahan said, "no, you can't talk me out of it."

Clint looked at Callahan, the other five men, then turned and walked back across the street.

EIGHT

"What'd he say?" Angel asked.

"I guess I should have let you go out the back door," Clint said.

"Nah," Angel said. "You're right. If I run, they'll just chase me."

Clint looked out the window. The six men were still there. Then he looked around the restaurant. It was empty. It seemed the citizens of Tucson knew when trouble was brewing. Even the street out front was deserted.

"They still there?" Angel asked.

"They are."

Clint turned, saw that Angel was seated at a table, drinking coffee.

"Any more of that?"

"Help yourself," Angel said. "The waiter brought it just before he ran out."

Clint poured himself a cup, then sat across from Angel.

"The fella across the street is named Big Ed Callahan," Clint said. "That name ring a bell for you?"

"Callahan? No."

"Never?"

"I said no," Angel replied. "Why?"

"I asked him why he wanted to kill you."

"And?"

"He said I should ask you."

Angel frowned.

"That's strange."

"I didn't get the names of any of the other men, but I don't think that matters," Clint said. "Callahan's the boss."

"Do you know who he is?"

"Never heard of him."

"Well," Angel said, "I guess I should go and find out who he is and why he wants to kill me."

"I'll go with you," Clint said. "I already told you the reason why."

"I won't try to talk you out of it."

"You any good with that hogleg on your hip?"

"I can hit what I shoot at," Angel said. "How do you want to play this?"

"Straight up," Clint said.

"How's that?"

"We walk out there and face them," Clint said. "I told them who I am. Maybe a couple of them will take the opportunity to walk away."

"You think so?"

"Depends on whether or not they believed me," Clint said, "and how afraid of their boss they are."

"Let's give them a few minutes to think, then," Angel said.

"Finish our coffee," Clint said.

"Boss?" Hunt asked.

"What?" Callahan said.

"You think he was tellin' the truth?"

"About what, Hunt?"

"About bein' the Gunsmith."

"What the hell would the Gunsmith be doin' with Tom Angel?" Callahan asked.

"I don't know," Angel said, "but what if it is really him?"

"I don't care," Callahan said. "I'm not going to let that change my plans."

"But, Ed, the men are kinda nervous."

"They should be," Callahan said. "It'll keep them on their toes."

"But . . . what do I tell them?"

"Tell them when Angel and the other fella—whoever he is—step out the door to spread out and put some distance between themselves."

"So we're gonna do this here?" Hunt asked.

"We're gonna do this here and now, Hunt," Callahan said. "Here and now. I want Tom Angel dead, do you hear me?"

"I hear you, boss."

"Then get them ready."

Hunt walked to the other men and told them what the boss had said.

"This is crazy," one of them said. "What if that really is the Gunsmith?"

"If it is," Hunt said, "we're all gonna earn the money Big Ed is payin' us, and we're gonna make big names for ourselves."

"Unless we're dead," the other man said.

"Then let's just make sure we ain't," Hunt said. "As soon as they come out the door, start shootin'."

NINE

"All right," Clint said, looking out the window, "they're still out there."

"How do they look?"

"Nervous," Clint said, "all but the boss. He's older, more experienced."

Angel came up next to Clint and looked out.

"How do you think they're gonna play it?" he asked.

"If they do what their boss says, he'll probably have them spread out, make some room between them. It's safer than bunching up."

"And if they don't listen to him?"

"Then they'll probably open fire as soon as they see us step outside."

"What do we do then?"

"Same thing they should be doing," Clint said. "Put some space between ourselves, and take cover."

"How do we divide them up?" Angel asked.

"I'll take Callahan, the boss," Clint said, "and the two to his right."

"So the three on the left are mine."

"Right."

"That's if they stand and shoot it out with us," Angel said.

"If it breaks down, and they start shooting as soon as we walk through the door, then it's every man for himself," Clint said. "Just start shooting."

"Yeah, okay."

"You nervous?" Clint asked.

"Would you be disappointed if I said yes?"

"No," Clint said. "If you didn't say yes, I'd say you were lying."

"Then I'm nervous."

"Good. You ready?"

"I'm ready."

They walked to the doorway.

"Okay, get ready," Callahan called out. "They're comin' out."

He stood straight up, instead of leaning against a post. He loosened his gun in his holster. This was finally going to happen. He kind of hoped that the other man actually was Clint Adams. He'd be known as the man who killed the Gunsmith.

He turned and looked at his men. He could see their nerves were on edge.

"First man who turns and runs, I'll kill myself," he told them. "Got it?"

"We got it, boss," Hunt said.

Callahan turned his eyes back to the door of the restaurant.

Hunt looked at the other men, said, "Spread out, and remember what I said."

"But the boss said to wait—"

"You wanna wait and give them a chance to kill us first?" Hunt asked. "What if that fella really is the Gunsmith?"

"He's right," one of the other men said.

"You all know I'm right," Hunt said. "Once Angel is dead, Big Ed Callahan ain't gonna complain about how it got done."

"Okay," the man said, and the others nodded.

"So spread out, and get ready," Hunt said. "As soon as they step out . . ."

"They're already spreading out," Clint said before they left the restaurant. "Be ready."

"I'm ready."

Clint stepped out, and Tom Angel followed a second later.

Clint saw the five men go for their guns immediately, and knew nobody was waiting.

"Draw!" he yelled to Angel.

Callahan felt the movement around him, knew his men were all going for their guns.

"What are you doin'?" he shouted, "What the hell are ya doin'?"

Their guns came out, and he knew they weren't stopping, and he didn't have any choice but to go with it. He could skin them alive when it was over.

"Make sure Angel is dead!" he shouted, drawing his own gun. "Angel's the one that's got to die first."

But at that moment, the five men didn't care who died first or last. As long as it wasn't them.

TEN

Clint dove to his right, firing at the same time, and firing accurately. His first shot hit Callahan in the shoulder, spinning him around and dumping him on his ass. His second shot hit one of the other men in the chest, killing him instantly. When Clint hit the ground, he rolled, came up between a couple of barrels, and used them as cover.

Angel dove to the right, hit the ground behind a horse trough, then peeked over it and fired twice. He missed once, but killed a man with his second shot. With Callahan down but only wounded, that left four men.

From his ass, Callahan saw Angel behind the horse trough. He only had eyes for him, didn't care where Adams was or what he was doing. Angel had to die, no matter what the cost.

He struggled to his feet, started across the street toward Angel.

Clint fired two more shots from behind the barrels, saw another man spin to the ground. He was aware of Angel firing to his left, but had no idea how accurate he was being.

There were three assailants left, including the wounded leader. The other two, seeing that their number had been cut in half, decided to run. That left only Callahan, who was staggering across the street toward Angel.

Clint stood up.

Callahan, unaware of the fact that his men were deserting him, continued across the street, firing at Angel. When the hammer kept falling on empty chambers, he simply continued to come, pulling the trigger over and over . . .

Angel, aware that Callahan was now out of bullets, stood up from behind the horse trough as the man continued to advance on him with his empty gun.

Clint, sure that Angel would not fire at the now unarmed man, began to eject his spent shells and replace them with live ones. When he was done, he figured they'd be able to question the man and find out why he was so eager to kill Angel.

Then he saw Angel pull the trigger . . .

Angel pointed his gun at Big Ed Callahan, thought about it for just a second, then pulled the trigger. He shot Callahan through the chest. The man staggered, blinked, and fell onto his face in the dirt . . .

As Big Ed fell into the street, Clint holstered his gun and said, "Jesus!"

Angel turned on Clint, his gun ready.

"Whoa!" Clint said, putting his hands up. "It's all over. The ones who aren't dead lit out."

Angel didn't respond.

"Why did you kill Callahan?" Clint asked. "We could have asked him some questions. Besides, he was out of bullets—"

Clint stopped when the blood began to leak from the corner of Angel's mouth. As the man fell toward him, the gun dropping from his hand, Clint caught him and lowered him gently to the ground.

He turned him over and looked for the wound, found it in Angel's abdomen. One of the first shots fired must have struck him.

"Tom, I'm sorry—" he started, but Angel grabbed hold of his arm and gripped it tightly.

"It's okay," he said, "you were right about not runnin'."

"Tell me . . . who should I contact? Where's your family?"

Angel opened his mouth as if to answer, but just then a great gout of blood erupted from his mouth, soaking the front of his shirt. He shuddered, and died.

From behind him, Clint heard somebody say, "You're in a lot of trouble, mister."

ELEVEN

"I told your friend to stay out of trouble," Sheriff Hastings said to Clint.

"And we had every intention of doing that, Sheriff."

"I don't call killing four men staying out of trouble, do you?"

"No, sir, I don't," Clint said, "but they didn't leave us much of a choice. And can I point out that my friend is also dead?"

"Just what was this all about anyway?"

"I have no idea," Clint said. He was sitting across the desk from the seated sheriff. The lawman had tried to take his gun, but Clint had refused to give it up. When he identified himself, the sheriff stopped trying to take it from him. "All I know is they tried to bushwhack him outside of town, and then came into town and tried to kill him again."

"And you killed them instead."

"I killed two of them. Tom killed two of them. The other two ran. But one of them killed him. I hope I don't have to keep pointing that out."

"No," the lawman said. "I know what happened out there."

"So now what?"

"I guess there's no reason for you to stay in town any longer," the sheriff said.

"That's not quite true."

"Why? What's to keep you here?"

"Well, for one thing, I want to try and find out who those six men were, and why they wanted to kill Tom Angel. And second, I need to find out where Angel was from, so I can tell his family that he's dead."

"How do you intend to do that?"

"By looking through all their belongings."

"Well," Hastings said, "all that stuff is over at the undertaker's, with the bodies."

"I'll go there, then," Clint said, rising to his feet.

"Okay," the sheriff said, "I suppose you can have a look." He stood up. "I'll take you over there."

"Thanks, Sheriff."

"You can thank me by leavin' my town as soon as you find out what you're lookin' for."

"Believe me," Clint said, "it'll be my pleasure to do just that."

The undertaker was named Grimes, a nondescript-looking man in his forties, with a sad face and only a few hairs on a freckled dome.

"The bodies are back there," he said, pointing to one room, "and their belongings are there," he added, pointing to another.

"I don't need to see the bodies," Clint said. "Just their belongings."

Grimes looked at Hastings.

"It's okay, Ben," the lawman said.

Grimes shrugged and motioned Clint to go ahead.

Clint went into the back room, which seemed to be for storage. Weapons and saddlebags were piled in a corner. He went over, knelt down, and began going through saddlebags. He found shirts—clean and dirty—tobacco, beef jerky, bullets, a Bible, and some letters. When he was finished, he left the room, taking all the letters with him.

"Find anything?"

"Letters," Clint said. "I'll have to read them to find out who's they are, and where they're from."

"When will you do that?" Hastings asked.

"Tonight, in my room," Clint said. "If I learn what I want, I'll be leaving town tomorrow morning."

"Well then," Hastings said, "let's hope you find out what you want."

"Agreed."

Clint left the undertaker's with the sheriff, and they split up from there. The lawman went back to his office, while Clint went to a saloon to have a drink in Tom Angel's memory.

Rather than wait until he got to his room, Clint took his beer to a back table and spread the letters out on the table. There were half a dozen, but they'd belonged to three of the men. Four letters were written to Callahan, apparently from his wife. She professed her love for him, told him that she missed him, but knew that he was doing what he had to do.

The fifth letter came from the saddlebags of a man named Kenneth Hunt. It was addressed to "Kenneth" but the letter began "Dear Kenny." It was from a girl, who said she was waiting for him, but knew he was doing what had to be done.

The letters were all sent to different towns, addressed to General Delivery.

None of the letters said why they were doing what they were doing.

The last letter had been written to Tom Angel.

TWELVE

Clint read the letter. As with the others, it was also written by a woman. It said:

> *Dear Tom,*
>
> *It's been several months since you left and I haven't heard from you. I'm hoping this letter will find you alive and well. Actually, I'm just hoping it will find you. I miss you so much, my love.*
>
> *Things have been crazy here since you left, and I know Mrs. Callahan has heard from Big Ed a few times. That's how I know you're not dead.*
>
> *Please know that I love you, and I hope that things can be cleared up before anyone else dies. Please write me and let me know how you are. I'll always love you.*
>
> *All My Love, Claire.*

The letter had been mailed from a town called Black Rock, Missouri.

Clint had been to Missouri many times—Saint Louis, Saint Joseph, a few other places—but had never heard of a place called Black Rock. At least, not in Missouri.

Clint reread the letters in his room that night, but didn't find out anything more. It was as if the letter writers were careful not to give away any information. He still had no idea who Callahan was, and why he'd wanted to kill Tom Angel.

Clint had breakfast before leaving town to head for Missouri. Over steak and eggs he realized that Tom Angel had been lying to him all along. Tom knew who Callahan was, and why he was after him. For some reason he hadn't wanted to tell Clint what it was all about. Maybe he thought if Clint knew, he wouldn't help him. Could it have been something that terrible?

Clint had a couple of reasons to go to Black Rock, Missouri. One was to tell Angel's family—or at least, Claire—what had happened to him. But the second reason was the more important to him.

Five men had died, and he'd killed two of them, but he didn't know why. Whenever he killed anyone, he had to know the reason. Otherwise it was for nothing, and that wasn't something he could accept.

When men died, there should be a reason—and a damned good one.

As Clint came out of the hotel, carrying his rifle and saddlebags, he saw Sheriff Hastings approaching.

"Good morning, Sheriff," he said. "Come to see me off?"

"Let's just say I wanted to make sure you got away safely."

"Might as well walk me to the stable, then."

They headed that way, side by side.

"Did you find out anythin' from those letters?" Hastings asked.

"A little bit," Clint said. "I didn't get any reasons, but I found out where I have to go."

The sheriff didn't ask where. It didn't matter to him. All that mattered was that Clint was leaving.

At the livery the sheriff stood aside and watched as Clint saddled Eclipse.

"What should I do with your friend's horse?" he asked.

"Sell it," Clint said. "The saddle, too. Use the money to pay for his burial."

"Okay. I'll see he gets a good send-off."

"Just put him in the ground, Sheriff."

"And the others?"

"I'm not concerned with them," Clint said. "They were trying to kill me. If you've got a boot hill, stick them there. You want to toss them into a mass grave together? Be my guest. Let them go to kingdom come together, the way they came to town and died."

Clint walked Eclipse outside, and mounted up.

"You might as well sell the horses and rigs of the other men, too," Clint said. "And their guns. Give the money to some poor families that could use it."

"That's a mighty fine idea, Adams," Hastings said. "I'll do it."

Clint nodded, turned Eclipse in the right direction.

"Sorry I couldn't be more hospitable to you, Adams," Hastings said.

"No problem, Sheriff," Clint said. "If our roles were reversed, I'd be feeling the same way."

"I appreciate that," Hastings said. "I wish you good luck."

"You, too," Clint said. "I hope there's no more trouble in your town."

"There's always gonna be trouble," Hastings said. "But maybe it's a ways off. Anyway, I can hope so."

"Good-bye to you," Clint said with a little salute.

THIRTEEN

It took Clint almost three weeks to cover the better than a thousand miles from Arizona to Missouri. He rode into Black Rock at midday, surprised to find the town was kind of large, and busy. A town this size—two banks, several hotels, and half a dozen saloons—was one he thought he would have heard of.

As he passed them, some of the buildings had both the look and the smell of fresh wood, as if they'd just recently sprung up.

He rode to the livery stable, handed Eclipse over to a youngster who seemed to form an immediate rapport with the big horse. Clint took his rifle and saddlebags and asked the boy about a hotel.

"You can't miss with any of 'em, sir," he said. "They're all clean and reasonable. You might wanna stay at the Mayflower, though. Got a good saloon and a steak house right across the street."

"Thanks," Clint said.

"And don't worry about your horse, sir," the boy said. "I'll take good care of him."

"Do you own this place?"

"No, sir, it's my pa's," he said, "but I pretty much take care of the horses. I'm real good with 'em."

"I can see that," Clint said. "Thanks again."

He took the boy's advice and registered at the Mayflower Hotel. He'd considered asking the boy about Tom Angel and a girl named Claire, but decided against it. His intention had been to talk with the local sheriff when he arrived, and he decided to stick to that plan.

He got a room that overlooked the main street and had no access from outside the window. That suited him just fine. He watched the street for a little while. The people appeared outgoing and energetic, greeting one another as they passed with a word or a gesture. A town that was on the rise, and happy about it. Even the desk clerk had been overly cheerful. What, Clint wondered, had happened to send Callahan and his men a thousand miles to try to catch and kill Tom Angel?

He freshened himself up with water from the pitcher and basin on the dresser, then strapped his gun back on and returned to the window. Just as the boy had told him, there was a steak house across the street, next to a saloon.

That's where he headed.

Midday was between meals for the townspeople, so Clint had no trouble picking out a table in the back.

"Steak, all the trimmings," he told the waiter. "Let 'er bleed."

"Yes, sir. To drink?"

Clint considered coffee, then said, "Beer, if it's cold."

"It's real cold, sir."

"Then bring it."

The beer was cold, the steak was bloody and tasty, the vegetables prepared just right. So far Black Rock was just too good to be true.

"Dessert, sir?"

"Only if the pie is as good as everything else."

"It is. Peach?"

"Apple."

"Good enough," the waiter said.

The waiter brought the pie and it was like silk.

"Who does the cooking?" Clint asked as he paid the bill.

"A big, fat, sweaty guy," the waiter said. "You don't wanna meet him. He ain't very friendly."

"Well, he doesn't have to be, the way he cooks," Clint said. "Thanks."

"Come back again, sir."

"I will."

Clint stepped out onto the street, looked around. A couple of well-dressed ladies walked past and said, "Good day." He tipped his hat to them. Then a couple of gents went by and nodded. He returned the nod.

He walked a few blocks before he came to the sheriff's office. He tried the door and found it locked. Knocking did no good. Obviously there was no one inside.

He turned and looked up and down the street. If the lawman was making his rounds, Clint should be able to find him just by walking the streets. That would also enable him to familiarize himself with the place.

He started walking, again exchanging greetings and nods with people who seemed very welcoming of strangers in their town.

He walked a few blocks again, then crossed over, found himself in front of a store that made him stop and look more closely. The window was filled with dresses, and on the window was stenciled the words CLAIRE'S DRESS SHOP.

FOURTEEN

For a moment he was stuck there. Could this be Tom Angel's Claire, who had sent him the letter? And if it was, should he go in and talk to her now? Or wait until he saw the sheriff?

He scanned the street, didn't see anybody wearing a badge. But a few doors away from the dress shop was a small saloon, so he decided to go in, have a beer, and maybe get some information about the local law.

As he entered the saloon, two men were coming out. They stepped aside to allow him to enter, and tipped their hats.

The interior of the salon was well lit, and about half full. But it was a small place, and didn't take that many bodies to fill it.

Clint went to the bar, where a smiling bartender was waiting for him. The man wore a boiled white shirt, a bow tie, and suspenders. His hair and mustache were impeccably trimmed.

"Help ya, friend?"

"A beer."

"Comin' up."

He drew the beer, leveled the head, and brought it over to Clint.

"Just get to town?" he asked.

"I did, yes."

"Well, first beer in town's on the house."

"Same rule in every saloon?"

"That's right."

"How do you know I haven't been to a few other saloons already?"

The man frowned.

"Why would you lie about that?" he asked.

"Never mind," Clint said. "This sure is a friendly little town."

"Little, maybe," the bartender said, "but it's growin'. And friendly? We sure are."

Clint drank down half his beer.

"You mind if I ask you a question?" he asked.

"I'm here to help," the bartender said.

"I'm looking for the sheriff," Clint said. "Went to his office, but it's locked."

"He must be out doin' his rounds."

"That's what I thought. Can you tell me what he looks like?"

"Sure," the bartender said. "You can't miss him. Sheriff Bodie is six-foot-six, got a big, bushy mustache. Need more?"

"No," Clint said, "that sure sounds like a man I'd notice."

"He's a good man."

"I'm sure this town would vote a good man into office."

"We sure did," the bartender said. "'Scuse me." He moved down the bar to serve another customer.

Clint worked on the remainder of the beer, wondering what further questions he should ask the bartender. Ask about Tom Angel? That might not be a good idea. Apparently, Angel had done something so bad the town had sent Ed Callahan after him. Or Callahan had taken it upon himself to chase him down and kill him. So maybe mentioning his name was not the way to go. But maybe he could ask about Callahan.

The bartender came back and said, "Sorry. You got more questions I can help ya with?"

"Yeah, maybe a few," Clint said. "You know Big Ed Callahan?"

"Everybody knows Big Ed," the man said. "He's well respected in this town."

"Any idea where I could find him?"

"Well, he's got a spread outside of town, about five miles east, but he ain't there right now."

"Oh? Where is he?"

"He's been out of town for a while."

"Do you know when he'll be back?"

"No idea."

"Is there anybody else out there I could talk to?" Clint asked.

"Sure. Big Ed's wife, and the ranch foreman. They could probably tell you somethin'."

"That's a good idea," Clint said. "Thanks."

"You, uh, ain't bringin' Mrs. Callahan no bad news, are ya?"

"What makes you ask that?"

"It's just that we here in town wouldn't want anythin' to upset her."

"Well," Clint said, "I can tell you that it's not my intention to say anything to upset her."

The bartender smiled broadly and said, "Well, that's good."

Clint finished his beer, set the empty mug down, and said, "Much obliged."

"Come on back."

"I will," Clint promised, and left.

FIFTEEN

Clint left the saloon, having decided that he'd asked enough questions in one place. He thought about a six-foot-six lawman and figured he shouldn't be so hard to find.

He went back to the sheriff's office, but the door was still locked. He walked the town in the other direction, and when he still didn't see the lawman on the streets, he decided that maybe he should be looking elsewhere—like inside.

He stopped in front of several restaurants and saloons, peering in the window for a large man wearing a badge, before he finally saw him. It had to be him, standing at the bar in a saloon called the Lucky Eight. He was standing so that Clint could see the badge on his chest. It would be too much of a coincidence for there to be two men that size in town . . . wearing a badge.

Clint entered the saloon and approached the man at the bar, who was deep in conversation with another man.

"Sam, I know about the problem and I'm lookin' into it," the sheriff was saying.

"Lookin' into it ain't good enough, Sheriff," the other

man said, who appeared to be a merchant. He was a short man in his fifties and was wearing a white apron. He could have been a butcher, but since the apron was clean, Clint assumed he ran the general store.

"Go back to your store, Sam," the sheriff said, "and I'll see you there later."

"Yeah, after you have a few more beers."

"Sam—" the bartender said warningly.

"Yeah, yeah, I know," Sam said. "I'm goin'."

Clint watched the man storm out. Apparently everyone in town wasn't interminably cheerful, and full of love for the local lawman.

Clint walked the rest of the way to the bar and stood next to the tall lawman.

"Help you?" the bartender asked.

"Actually," Clint said, "I was looking for Sheriff Bodie here."

"For me?" the man with the badge asked. "What's on your mind, friend?"

"Well, first I'd like to get a beer."

"First one in town's on the house," the bartender said.

"I know. I already had one on the house in another saloon."

The bartender set the beer in front of Clint, looking surprised.

"Well, well," Bodie said, "we got us an honest man in town, Teddy. You give him this beer on the house anyway."

"Sure, Sheriff."

"And give me another one," Bodie said. He looked at Clint. "You wanna sit down?"

"Sure."

The lawman accepted his fresh beer, led Clint to a back table.

"Mind if I ask your name?" Bodie said as they sat.

"I don't mind at all, Sheriff," Clint said. "I'm Clint Adams."

"That a fact?"

"It's a fact."

"The Gunsmith? For real and true?"

"You want me to shoot something to prove it?" Clint asked.

"No, no," Bodie said. "Only a fool would claim to be you. That'd be painting a target on any man's back."

The man had a point there.

"What can I do for you?" the sheriff asked. "What brings you to Black Rock?"

"Actually," Clint said, "Ed Callahan and Tom Angel."

The sheriff's face froze.

"What do you know about them?"

"I know they're both dead."

The big man leaned forward.

"When?"

"A few weeks ago."

"Where?"

"Tucson."

"I didn't hear anythin'," Bodie said, "or read anythin' in the newspapers."

"Why would you?" Clint asked. "Neither man is particularly famous."

"How did it happen?"

"In the street," Clint said. "Callahan and five other men tried to shoot Angel down."

"And he took them?"

"He did," Clint said, "with my help. But he got killed doing it."

"You killed Mr. Callahan?"

"I killed two of his boys," Clint said. "Angel killed Callahan."

"Who killed Angel?"

"Don't know," Clint said. "Didn't see whose bullet hit him."

Bodie sat back, looking unhappy.

"This ain't good," he said. "Mr. Callahan was well respected around here."

"And Tom Angel?"

Bodie didn't answer right away. He eyed Clint for a few moments.

"What do you know about Angel?"

"Nothing."

"Why'd you help him, then?"

"The first time I saw him, he was pinned down behind a fallen tree. Callahan and his men were trying to kill him. I saw one man against six, and I took a hand."

"Got him out of that mess?"

"Right, without firing a shot. But then we went to Tucson, and Callahan and his bunch showed up. They didn't give us any choice."

"I can check this story with the sheriff in Tucson, you know," Bodie said.

"Be my guest," Clint said. "His name is Hastings."

"Hastings."

"Look," Clint said, "what was this all about? I'd like to know why I ended up killing men I didn't know."

Bodie shoved his chair back.

"We can talk about that later," he said. "I've got somethin' I've got to do."

He stood up and started away.

"Now, wait a minute," Clint said, chasing after him. They got outside before Bodie stopped and turned to face him.

"I need to know what's going on," Clint said.

"What's going on is you poked your nose in somebody else's business," Bodie said.

"It's always my business when somebody's outnumbered," Clint said.

"Look," Bodie said, "I told you we'll talk more later."

"Well, tell me this," Clint said. "The Claire who runs that dress shop down the street. She belong to Tom Angel?"

"*Belong* is a strong word."

"Well, he got a letter from a Claire," Clint said. "That's how I traced him here. Would that be her?"

"Yeah," Bodie said, "yeah, that's her."

"There any reason I shouldn't talk to her?" Clint asked.

"I suppose not," Bodie said. "I guess if I told you not to, you'd go ahead anyway."

"You guess right," Clint said. "What about Mrs. Callahan?"

"What about her?" Sheriff Bodie seemed to get even tenser.

"Well, I'd like to talk to her," Clint said. "Where does she—"

"Look here," Bodie said, poking Clint in the chest with a thick finger, "don't go bothering Mrs. Callahan, you hear?"

"I don't want to bother her," Clint said. "I just want to tell her that her husband is dead. And find out why he was trying to kill Tom Angel."

"I got things to do, Adams," Bodie said. "I'll see you later about all this."

"Yeah, okay," Clint said. "We'll talk later. But know this . . . I'm not leaving town until I know what the hell this is all about."

Bodie stared at him, then turned and stalked away.

* * *

When Sheriff Bodie got to his office, he slammed the door
and sat behind his desk. He was going to have to ride out
to the Callahan ranch, but not in broad daylight. He'd have
to wait until after dark to go out and see Angela Callahan
and tell her about her husband. He didn't relish the job.

SIXTEEN

Ray Winston watched Angela Callahan take off her dress and set it down on a chair, then remove her undergarments until she was totally naked.

She was a tall woman with large, pear-shaped breasts. Her dark nipples stood out in sharp contrast to her pale skin. And between her lovely thighs was a tangle of dark hair that was even blacker than the hair on her head. She was a beautiful woman married to a man twenty years older than her, which was why she had the foreman—five years younger than she was—in her bed.

Winston was already naked, reclining on the bed she shared with her husband—when he was around.

"Oh my," she said, gliding into the bed until her nose was pressed into his crotch, "you are glad to see me, aren't you?"

"You bet I am," Winston said. "It's been days."

She closed her hand around his giant, hard cock and said, "I've been busy, Ray. You know I've got to run things when Big Ed isn't around."

"And I told you I'm here to help you with that."

"Ray," she said, licking the head of his cock, "you help me with this. I don't need you to help me with business. You don't have a head for it." She licked him again. "This is the only head I'm interested in."

He opened his mouth to protest but she opened her mouth and took half his cock into it. He gasped while she wet him, then started to bob up and down on him, sucking him noisily.

He was never as happy as he was when he was fucking the boss's wife, but he sure wished she'd let him help her with other parts of her life.

Clint watched the tall lawman stride away, then turned and walked down the street to the dress shop. But he'd waited too long, and when he tried the door, it was locked. He peered inside, didn't see anyone, but knocked on the door anyway.

The store had probably only just closed. If Claire didn't live upstairs, she was probably on the street going home, or having supper somewhere. He should have asked Bodie what she looked like, but maybe the lawman wouldn't have told him.

On the other side of the dress shop was the general store.

Clint walked over there, saw that the front door was still open. He went inside.

Sam, the irate man wearing the apron, was behind the counter, writing something down.

"Still open?" Clint asked.

"Just barely," Sam said. "Just ain't had time to close the door yet." He looked up. "What can I—say, didn't I see you in the saloon?"

"You did. I talked to the sheriff after you did."

"Did you get any satisfaction?" the man asked. "Because I sure didn't."

"That's funny," Clint said. "I was told that everyone liked Sheriff Bodie. In fact, it seems like everybody in town likes everybody else."

"Oh yeah, that's what they'd like you to think," Sam said. But at that moment he suddenly looked as if he realized he'd said something wrong. "Wait a minute, who are you?"

"My name is Clint Adams."

"Adams," Sam said. "Clint Adams? You mean . . . the Gunsmith?"

"That's right."

The color drained from the man's face and he looked frightened for his life.

"Oh, uh, wait," he said, "I didn't mean—I wasn't sayin' anythin' . . . I love this town. Tell 'em I like everybody!"

"Take it easy," Clint said. "Nobody sent me here. I came here on my own. I only just got into town."

"W-Well," Sam said, "whataya want?"

"I wanted to ask you about the woman who runs the dress shop next to you."

"Claire?" he asked with relief. "You want to ask me about Claire?" The color flooded back into his face.

"Yes," Clint said. "I'd like to talk to her, and her shop is closed."

"She—She must've just closed," Sam said. "Normally I'd be closed by this time, too."

"Can you tell me where to find her?" Clint asked. "Where she lives?"

"Well . . . I don't know if I should tell you where she lives, since you're a stranger," Sam said. Now that he seemed convinced that Clint wasn't going to kill him, he had a lot more confidence. "Why don't you wait until she opens in the morning?"

"I'd really like to see her today," Clint said. "Can you tell me where she eats?"

"Ah, yes," Sam said, "She does stop to eat on her way home, usually at the small place a few blocks away called Jenny's Café."

"Which way?"

"Go out and to the right. She's probably still there eating because she closes up the same time every night."

"What does she look like?"

"Oh, uh, she's really pretty, kinda young, with straight, long dark hair and a great smile."

"Okay, thanks." Clint started to leave, then stopped. He turned, and as he did, Sam seemed startled, and jumped back a step.

"Can I ask you a question?"

"Huh? Sure."

"What was it you were complaining to the sheriff about?"

"Complaining?" Sam asked. "I wasn't complaining. The sheriff and I were just, uh, kiddin' around. We do that a lot."

"Okay," Clint said, knowing the man was lying and still scared. "Thanks."

"Sure thing, Mr. Adams," Sam said. "Sure thing."

Clint left, feeling bad for having frightened the man.

After Clint Adams left, Sam Barrett rushed to the door, closed it, and locked it, then pressed his back to it and breathed a sigh of relief. He might have just literally dodged a bullet. Even if the Gunsmith was not there to kill him, he had learned his lesson. He was going to keep his big mouth shut from now on.

SEVENTEEN

Clint walked a few blocks and came to the café with JENNY'S over the door. As he entered, he saw that the place was small, and crowded. It was obviously a very popular restaurant in town.

He looked around the room, saw more than one pretty young woman, but only one of them had long, straight dark hair, and was sitting alone. He felt sure this was Tom Angel's Claire.

Now he had to decide if he wanted to tell her Angel was dead while she was eating her dinner in a room crowded with people. He decided the answer was no. There were bound to be tears and why should he hit her with that kind of news, and embarrass her at the same time?

"Sir?" a waiter said. "If you'll wait a few minutes, I can seat you."

"That's okay," Clint said. "I'll try again later. But it smells great in here."

"Thank you, sir," the man said, and hurried to help some of his diners.

Clint turned to leave, but at that moment a woman in

her thirties came out of the kitchen and looked right at him. Their eyes met. She was attractive in a very earthy way, and held his eyes boldly for a few seconds before looking away. She walked across the room to join Claire at her table.

Clint stepped outside.

Claire Collins ate her beef stew slowly, without tasting it very much. Jenny Pool, who owned and operated Jenny's, came over and sat with her. She was an older woman who had taken Claire under her wing when she first arrived in town several years before.

"What's wrong, sweetie?" Jenny asked.

"Is it obvious?" Claire asked.

"Yes," Jenny said. "You're very down."

"I know," Claire said. "I just . . . I'm just waiting for Tom to come back."

"Oh, honey," Jenny said, putting her hand on Claire's, "do you really think he will?"

"With Mr. Callahan after him, I'm afraid not," Claire said, "but I still keep looking down the street for him to come riding back."

"I guess I don't blame you, honey," Jenny said, patting the girl's hand.

"I'm sorry," Claire said. "The food is great, as usual."

"Yeah, yeah," Jenny said. "Hey, did you see the man who came in a few minutes ago?"

"No," Claire said. "What about him?"

"Well, he's a stranger in town, I could tell that."

"And?"

"And he wasn't exactly handsome, but he was very . . . he had a presence, you know?"

"So you liked what you saw, huh?"

"Well," Jenny said, "we sort of looked at each other. I think we had a connection."

Claire looked around.

"So where is he?"

"He left," Jenny said.

"But why?"

"Well, we're kind of busy," she said. "But he spoke briefly to Al, so maybe I'll find out what he said."

"Call Al over," Claire said excitedly, "and let's find out."

Jenny grinned at her friend and said, "Okay."

She waved the waiter over.

EIGHTEEN

Clint found himself a spot across the street in front of another store that had already closed, and waited. Having decided to let the girl eat in peace, he now had to decide whether he should approach her on the street, or follow her home and then knock on her door. Stopping her on the street might frighten her, and he'd already scared enough people that day.

He leaned against a post and folded his arms, eyes on the front of the café. He found himself thinking about the woman whose eyes he had met, wondering if she was Jenny.

"He didn't say much," Al, the waiter, told the two women.

"Well, tell us what he did say," Jenny said.

"I told him I could seat him if he waited," Al said. "He said it smelled great in here, but he couldn't wait. He said he'd come back later."

"Okay, Al," Jenny said. "Thanks."

Al had been working for Jenny for a year. He was in

his fifties, and tried to advise her on her business and her life.

"Don't either one of you think about getting involved with him," he advised now.

"Why not?" Jenny asked.

"He's a gunman."

"How can you tell that?" Claire asked.

"Because I've seen his type come and go," Al said. "You can tell by the way he wears his gun."

"Okay, Al," Jenny said. "Thanks."

He went to take care of his diners.

"Do you think he's right?" Claire asked. "The man is a gunman?"

"I don't know."

"Why would a gunman be in Black Rock?" the younger woman asked. "And why would he come in here?"

"Maybe he came here to eat," Jenny said. "What he's doing in town, I don't know."

"I just hope—"

"What?"

"If he is a gunman," Claire said, "I hope he's not here about Tom."

Jenny didn't have an answer for that, so she just took her friend's hand.

Clint pushed away from the post when he saw Claire come walking out of the restaurant. He started across the street, but stopped when he saw Jenny standing in the doorway. She was watching him, and would know if he started following Claire. While he meant her no harm, following her might alarm the other woman.

Instead of following Claire, he decided to cross the street and talk to Jenny—if that's who she was.

"Are you Jenny?" he asked.

"That's right," she said. "You weren't looking for a table when you came in, were you?"

"No, ma'am," he said. "I was looking for a girl named Claire. Was that her who just left?"

"Yes, it was. What do you want with her?"

"I have some bad news for her," Clint said, "but maybe I should talk to you first. Are you her friend?"

"I'm her best friend," Jenny said. Her arms had been folded beneath her full breasts, but now she dropped them to her sides. Is this about Tom?"

"Tom Angel, yes, ma'am."

"Why don't you come in?" she asked. "I'll give you some coffee and we can talk."

NINETEEN

"He's dead, isn't he?" Jenny asked a few moments later. They each had a cup of coffee in front of them.

"Yes, ma'am."

"Okay," she said, "you've got to stop calling me 'ma'am.' What's your name?"

"Clint Adams."

"Al was right," she said, more to herself, but he heard her.

"What?"

"Oh, my waiter, Al," she said. "He told us you were a gunman."

"I'm not a gunman."

"You're the Gunsmith, right?"

"That's right."

"But not a gunman?"

"No."

"But your reputation—"

"You can't believe everything you hear, or read," he said. "Call me Clint. What should I call you?"

"Just call me Jenny."

"All right, Jenny," Clint said.

"So tell me," she said. "How did you know Tom Angel? How did he die?"

"He was shot."

"By Ed Callahan?"

"Or one of his men. He had five with him."

"And where are they?"

"Three of them are dead. The other two ran off."

Jenny sat back in her chair. They were seated at the same table Claire had been sitting at. The look on her face was one of shock.

"Did you know Callahan?" Clint asked.

"Everybody around here knew Big Ed."

"But did you know him personally?"

"He ate here occasionally, and we spoke. But I can't say that I knew him very well."

"How about his men?"

"Some of them have eaten here, too, but—"

"His wife?"

"I've never met her. You haven't told me how you knew Tom."

"Well . . . I was with him when he was shot. In fact, they were shooting at me, too."

"This sounds like a good story," she said. "How about a beer?"

"That sounds great."

Over a beer, and while the restaurant emptied out, Clint told her about how he had come upon Angel being shot at, and about what happened later in Tucson.

"That's a wild story," she said.

"You don't believe me?"

"No, no, I do believe you," she said. "Why would you lie?"

"I wouldn't," Clint said. "Jenny, can you tell me why Ed Callahan was so anxious to kill Tom Angel?"

"I don't know," she said. "I have no idea."

"But somebody in town knows, right?"

"I suppose so," she said. "Maybe the sheriff?"

"Or Callahan's wife?" he asked.

"Maybe."

"What about Claire?"

"I don't think she'd know," Jenny said.

"How close was she to Tom?"

"Very close," Jenny said. "She was in love with him."

"Was he in love with her?"

Jenny frowned, then said, "I suppose so."

"You suppose so?"

"Well, she confides in me, but she's never told me that he said that."

"I found a letter on him, from her," Clint said. "That's how I tracked him down to here."

"He carried her letter?"

I nodded.

"Then he must have loved her," she said. "That's going to make the news harder for her to take."

"I'm going to have to tell her," Clint said. "Can you tell me where she lives?"

"I'll do better than that," she said. "I'll take you there."

"If you just give me directions—"

"If you tell her the man she loves is dead," Jenny said, "she's gonna need a friend, don't you think?"

"You're right."

"Let me just tell the cook I'm going," she said. "I'll be right back."

She got up and hurried to the kitchen, while Clint remained seated and finished his beer. It would be a good idea to have her along when he gave Claire the news. He wasn't all that comfortable with weeping women.

TWENTY

Claire lived in a small house situated in an area among other, larger houses.

"She owns her own house?" he asked.

"Actually," Jenny said, "she rents it. It's just a two-room shack, really, that one of the other home owners fixed up to rent."

They approached the front door and Jenny knocked. When the door opened, Claire was obviously surprised to see Jenny in Clint's company.

"Jenny."

"Claire, can we come in?"

Claire looked past Jenny at Clint.

"This is Clint Adams," Jenny said. "He wants to talk to you . . . about Tom."

"Tom?" Claire said. "Is he all right?"

"Claire," Jenny said, "let us come in."

Claire stepped aside and allowed them to enter.

The inside was clean, sparsely furnished.

"Please," Claire said, "sit down."

Jenny sat on a small divan, while Clint sat on an arm-chair. Claire remained standing.

"Claire," Jenny said, "you better sit down."

"Oh, God," Claire said, and lowered herself into the other armchair.

"Claire," Clint said, because he didn't know her last name, "I'm sorry, but Tom Angel is dead."

A tear fell from one eye. She sat very still.

"H-How?"

Clint told her how he'd met Angel, and how he ended up being shot.

"Mr. Callahan and his men?" she asked.

"Callahan and three of his men are dead," Clint said. "Tom and I killed them."

"I'm glad."

"Claire," Clint said, "do you know why Ed Callahan was so eager to kill Tom that he'd chase him a thousand miles with five men?"

"I—I don't know."

"You must know something," he said. "How did you know how to get a letter to him?"

"My letter?" she said. "He got my letter?"

"He did," Clint said. "That's how I found you."

"Where is it?" she demanded. "Where's my letter?"

Clint took the folded letter from his shirt pocket and handed it to her. She clutched it to her chest.

"Claire," Clint said, "I killed two men trying to help Tom. I'd like to find out why."

"I don't know," she said. "I can't help you."

"But you must—"

"Please!" she said stridently. "Please leave before I em-barrass myself in front of you."

Clint looked at Jenny, who nodded at him. He decided

to leave the girl to her grief, and return another time to question her further.

"I'm sorry," he said, standing and heading for the door.

"Claire," Jenny said, "do you want me to stay?"

"N-No," Claire said, "I'll be fine. I—I'll talk to you tomorrow, Jenny."

"All right," Jenny said.

She followed Clint to the door. They went outside and pulled the door closed behind them.

Outside, Clint said, "She must know something."

"Why would she lie?"

"I don't know," Clint said. "Maybe she knows something and doesn't know it."

"Well," Jenny said, "we won't find out tonight."

"Maybe I can talk to her again tomorrow," he said.

"Come on," she said, "I'll walk you back to town."

When they reached her restaurant, the door was closed but not locked.

"I'd better go in and help clean up," Jenny said. "Would you like something to eat?"

"No, thanks," Clint said, "but I'll try your restaurant tomorrow, if that's okay."

"Of course," she said. "What do you intend to do tomorrow? I mean, other than talk to Claire again?"

"I'm going to ride out to the Callahan ranch and talk to Mrs. Callahan."

"That should be interesting."

"Why do you say that?"

"Have you talked to anyone else in town?"

"Bartenders, and the sheriff."

"Find out anything about Mrs. Callahan?"

"No," I said. "In fact, the sheriff was talking to me pretty willingly until I told him why I was here."

"Well, she's an interesting woman."

"I thought you didn't know her."

"I don't," she said, "not well, but you don't have to know her to know she's interesting. There are a lot of stories."

"What kind of stories?"

"I think I should let you form your own opinions."

"Come on," Clint said, "give me the dirt."

She laughed and said, "Aren't you the man who told me not to believe everything you read, or hear?" She opened the door. "I'll see you tomorrow."

She slipped inside before he could ask her anything else.

TWENTY-ONE

Clint stopped in the Lucky Eight for a few beers. The bartender's name was Willie. He told Clint where there was a place he could still get a meal.

Before turning in, Clint went to the café Willie recommended and had a bad meal. He didn't know why he had refused Jenny's offer of a meal at her place, but he was certainly going to try her café the next day.

He went back to the Lucky Eight for one more beer.

"How was your meal?" Willie asked.

"Terrible."

"Well, I didn't say it was good," Willie said, "I said it was still open."

Clint accepted his last beer from the bartender.

"Tell me about Sheriff Bodie," he said.

"What's to tell?"

"How long has he been sheriff?"

"A few years."

"What kind of a lawman is he?"

Willie hesitated, looked around, and then said, "He's okay."

"Just okay?"

"Well, there's lots of folks who like him," the bartender said, "but there's some who don't."

"Like Sam?"

"Sam?" Willie asked. "Oh, you mean Sam Barrett, from the general store?"

"He didn't seem too happy with the sheriff when I was in here earlier."

"Sam's just a little upset, that's all," Willie said. "Seems somebody's been breakin' into his store at night, leavin' a mess."

"And the sheriff hasn't done anything?"

"Well, the sheriff figures it's just kids," Willie said. "See, the only thing that ever gets took is some of Sam's rock candy."

"I see. Willie, I want to ask you something else, and if you don't want to answer, you don't have to."

Willie leaned on his elbows and said, "Well, I'll answer if I can. What is it?"

"What do you know about Ed Callahan and Tom Angel?"

Willie stood up straight.

"What you wanna go and ask about them for?"

"You know them?" Clint said.

"I'm acquainted with both of them."

"Then do you know why Big Ed—"

"No. I don't know nothing. Why don't you ask them what they got against each other," Willie said. "I don't meddle in other folks' affairs."

"I was just wondering—"

"I'm sorry," the bartender said, "I got some work to do."

"Sure."

He hurried to the other end of the bar, where he started talking earnestly to another man standing there. Every so often they'd look over Clint's way. He figured it was time to go to his hotel, and left.

Sheriff Bodie left town on horseback after dark and rode out to the Callahan spread. He reined in his horse behind the barn, tied him off, and made his way quietly to the bunkhouse. He could hear snoring from inside. He entered quietly, lit a match, and looked at the men sleeping in their beds. One bed was empty. It was located at the far end of the room, away from the others, and belonged to Ray Winston, the foreman of the ranch.

He moved back toward the door, gently shook the man who was sleeping closest to it.

"What the—" Eddie Beckman said, squinting up at the big lawman.

"Outside," Bodie hissed.

He stepped outside, waited a few moments for Eddie to come stumbling out.

"What the hell, Sheriff?" Eddie whined. "I was sleepin'."

"I'm lookin' for Ray," Bodie said. "Where is he?"

"Where d'ya think he is?" Eddie asked. "The boss is away, so Eddie's up at the big house most of the time. Lookin' ta get himself killed, if ya ask me. The boss comes back and find him up there . . ."

"The house, huh?"

"That's right."

Well, Bodie thought, there wasn't much chance of the boss coming back and catching him, but he didn't tell Eddie that.

"Okay, Eddie, go on back to bed."

"What's it all about, Sheriff?"

"Never mind, Eddie," Bodie said. "Just go back to bed like I told you."

"Well, hell," Eddie whined, "seems if'n ya wake a man outta a dead sleep, ya oughtta tell him what the hell is goin' on."

But he went back inside, closing the door gently behind him.

Bodie hesitated, then shrugged and started walking up to the big house.

TWENTY-TWO

Inside the house, Ray Winston was eagerly driving his cock into the boss's wife, who had her legs spread as far as she could, holding her own ankles in her hands.

"Oh, yeah," she gasped, "oh baby, yeah." When she was in bed with her husband, it was missionary position, some grunts and groans, a squirt, and then he'd roll over and go to sleep. There was nothing like having a young man between her legs.

She was about to tell him to flip her over so he could fuck her from behind when they both heard someone knocking on the door downstairs.

"Goddamnit!" Ray swore. "Whoever that is, I'll kill 'im."

"Don't answer it," Angela whispered into his ear.

"I gotta," he said. "I can't concentrate with that banging."

He withdrew from her, his cock red and raging.

"Whoever it is," she said, "make them go away."

"I'll make them dead," he said, pulling on his shirt and trousers. "I'll be right back."

* * *

When the door opened, Bodie stepped back. Winston was not as large as he was, but the man's obvious anger drove him back.

"Jesus, Bodie. Whataya want?"

"We got problems, Ray."

"What kind of problems?"

"The dead kind."

"What the hell are you talking about?"

"Big Ed is dead."

Winston stared at him, then asked, "What?"

"Dead."

"How do you know?"

"A man who was there told me."

"And what about Angel?"

"Dead, too."

"And the others?"

"Three are dead," Bodie said. "The other two ran off."

"Jesus," Winston said. "Okay, yeah. You better come in and tell her."

Angela Callahan sat on a sofa in the living room, her luscious body wrapped in a robe. She listened while Bodie told her what Clint Adams had told him.

"And this is Clint Adams?" she said. "The Gunsmith?"

"That's right."

"And how do we know he's telling the truth?" she asked.

"I sent a telegram to the sheriff in Tucson," Bodie said. "He answered right away It's all true."

"Who killed my husband?"

"According to Adams, it was Angel."

"Tom . . ." she said, shaking her head.

"Who killed Angel?" Winston asked.

"He ain't sure," Bodie said. "There was a lot of lead flyin' around."

"It was probably Big Ed," Angela said. "He wouldn't want anyone else to do it."

"What should we do?" Bodie asked. "He wants to come out here and talk to you."

"Get him out of town," Winston said.

"No," Angela said. "No, let him come."

"What?" Winston asked.

She looked at the foreman.

"I want to talk to him."

"Angela—"

"See the sheriff out, Ray," she said.

"Okay," Winston said. "I'll be right back."

"No," she said, "I'm tired, Ray, and I have to think. I'll see you tomorrow."

Winston had thrown on his clothes, had his gun belt in his hand, so there was no reason he couldn't just leave.

Except that he didn't want to.

"Angela," he said, "you shouldn't be alone—"

"Tomorrow, Ray," she said. "For now just go."

"Yeah, okay," Winston said. "Come on, Bodie."

He led the sheriff from the room and out of the house.

Angela stood up, went to a sideboard against the wall, and got herself a glass of whiskey. Big Ed was dead. That meant everything was hers. Finally.

Outside, Winston said to Bodie, "Just try it my way once."

"Your way?"

"Yeah," the foreman said, "see if you can get him to leave town. Talk to Harvey. He'll handle it."

"Okay, Ray," Bodie said, "but it's your idea, right?"

"That's right, Sheriff," Winston said, "it's my idea."

TWENTY-THREE

Clint woke the next morning with the bad food from the night before weighing heavily in his stomach. He decided to remedy that by going to have breakfast at Jenny's. He poured some water into the basin on the dresser and washed himself thoroughly, feeling he didn't have the time or the patience for a bath at the moment. Satisfied that he was as clean as he was going to get, he dressed and left his room.

Down in the lobby he found trouble . . .

A half hour earlier, six men had entered the hotel lobby, and one of them had walked to the front desk.

"There's a stranger in town," he said to the clerk. "What room is he in?"

"I can't tell ya that, Harvey," the clerk said. "I'd lose my job."

"Kid," Harvey Tracy said, "you're gonna lose more than your job if you don't—"

"Harvey," Simon Fuller said, putting his hand on his friend's arm, "don't threaten the kid. He's just doin' his job. The fella's got to come down sometime this mornin', right?"

"Yeah, that's right," Harvey said. "So we'll wait for him to come down."

"And do what?" one of the other men asked.

"Let him know he better leave town," Harvey said. "We don't want his kind here."

"What kind is that?" the desk clerk asked.

Harvey turned on him and said, "A troublemaker!"

The clerk had to keep himself from grinning. These fellers obviously had no idea who the stranger was. All they had to do was look in the register, but he surreptitiously removed the book from the counter and put it underneath.

He couldn't wait to see their faces when they found out who they were dealing with.

"All right," Harvey called out to the other men, "we're gonna wait here for him to come down."

"How long do we wait?"

"As long as it takes," Harvey said. "We got to get this done today."

The other men shrugged and they all settled down to wait.

Clint came down the stairs, saw the armed men standing in the lobby. One of them he recognized from the saloon, the man the bartender had been talking to at the end of the bar.

When he reached the lobby, the men turned and looked at him.

"Hey, you!" the one he recognized from the saloon called.

"Who are you?" Clint asked.

"My name's Harvey Tracy," the man said, "and we're here to help you mount up and ride out of town."

"Is that a fact?"

Clint looked over at the clerk, who was leaning on the desk with his chin in his hand. He seemed to be enjoying himself.

"We'll walk you to the livery and help you saddle up. It's time for you to leave town."

Clint looked at the six men, all of whom seemed intent on trying to intimidate him with their looks.

"I don't think so," he said.

"What?" Harvey asked.

"I'm not ready to leave town, but thanks for the offer of help," Clint said. He started past the men.

"Hey, wait a minute," Harvey said. "There are six of us standin' here, and one of you." Obviously, the man didn't understand why Clint wasn't intimidated.

"Yeah? So?"

"Maybe you don't understand, partner," Harvey said. "We're tellin' you to leave town."

"I understand perfectly."

"Well, good," Harvey said. "So then, you're leavin', right?"

"Wrong," Clint said. "I'm not leaving."

Harvey leaned in and said loudly, as if Clint were hard of hearing, "There's six of us."

Clint looked at each of the six men in turn and asked, "And how many of you are willing to die just to try to get me to leave town?"

The man stared back at him.

One man leaned over and said to Simon Fuller in a loud whisper, "Who is this guy?"

Simon realized at that point that nobody had bothered to ask.

TWENTY-FOUR

Whoever he was, Simon thought, he obviously wasn't bothered by six men standing in front of him, wearing guns.

"Harvey—" Simon started.

"What?" Harvey asked. "What is it, Simon?"

"Why don't we find out who he is?" Simon asked. "Before we start somethin'."

"Your friend is showing some sense," Clint said.

"I don't care who he is," Harvey said, then turned to Clint and said, "I don't care who you are."

"Maybe they do," Clint said, indicating the other five men.

The desk clerk was smiling openly now.

"Mister," Harvey said, "you're gonna step out on that street and face six men. What do you think of that?"

"It won't be the first time," Clint said. "In fact, it won't even be the first time this year. Let's go."

"Wait, wait, wait," Simon said, grabbing Harvey's arm now. "What's goin' on? This guy ain't afraid, Harvey. You said he'd be afraid when he saw how many of us there are."

"He's too stupid to be afraid."

"I don't think that's it," the desk clerk called out.

Harvey turned and shouted, "What do you know about it?"

"Well," the clerk said happily, "for one thing I know his name."

"I don't care—" Harvey started, but Simon cut him off abruptly.

"What's his name?" he asked.

The clerk brought the register out and slapped it down on the desk.

"It's in the book."

Simon walked to the desk, opened the book, and looked. Then he turned and stared at Clint, before looking at Harvey.

"Damn you, Harvey!" he said.

"Can I go now?" Clint asked. "Is this over?"

"It's over," Simon said. "We're sorry, Mr. Adams."

"What? Wait, no, it ain't over," Harvey said.

"Adams, Harvey," Simon yelled. "His name is Clint Adams!"

Harvey frowned and said, "What?"

"The goddamned Gunsmith!" Simon said.

"What?" one of the other men said.

"Jesus Christ!" another said.

"I ain't facin' no Gunsmith!" a third man said.

"I'm outta here," the fourth man said.

"Wait for me," the first said.

"Hey, wait," Harvey said. "It don't matter who he is."

"Who are you kiddin', Harvey?" Simon asked as Clint went out the door. "That man could kill all six of us without breakin' a sweat."

"You're talkin' about his reputation," Harvey said. "That can't kill you."

"I'm talkin' about the man himself," Simon said. "If you want to face him, you can do it by yourself."

"I will," Harvey said. "I'll show all of you he's just a man."

Harvey went out the door after Clint.

Clint was crossing the street when he heard Harvey yell behind him, "Adams!"

He turned. The man was standing in the street, feet spread, arms hanging down.

"I don't care who you are. You're leavin' town."

"Don't be a fool," Clint said. "You're all alone."

"I been alone before."

"But you've never been dead before," Clint said. "If you go for that gun, you'll leave me no choice but to kill you."

"You can't make a fool out of me and then just walk away," Harvey said.

"Better I make a fool of you than I make you dead, Harvey. Think about it."

He could see by the man's eyes that he *was* thinking about it. He only hoped he made the right decision.

"Hold it!"

Both men turned and saw Sheriff Bodie walking toward them with long, purposeful strides.

"Get back, Sheriff," Harvey said. "This ain't none of your affair."

"Harvey," the big man said, "stand down before I slap you down."

"Listen to him, Harvey," Clint said. "He's saving your life."

"Goddamn it!"

Harvey looked like he was about to go for his gun, but Bodie was on him, clubbing him over the head with a massive fist. The man slumped to the ground, and as he fell, Bodie plucked his gun from his holster.

The big lawman turned to Clint and said, "Go on about your business, Adams."

"I was just going to breakfast, Sheriff." He turned and walked away.

TWENTY-FIVE

Jenny greeted Clint herself at the door, took him to a back table.

"Have you seen Claire today?" he asked as he sat down.

"No," she said, "not since last night. If she doesn't come in, I'll have to go and see if she's at home, or at her store."

"I hope she's all right."

"What can I get you today?" she asked.

"Steak and eggs."

"Biscuits? Coffee?"

"Of course."

"Comin' up."

She went to the kitchen, came back almost immediately with a basket of warm biscuits, a coffeepot, and a mug. As she was setting them down, Sheriff Bodie came in. He walked directly to Clint's table, towering over Jenny.

"Is there gonna be trouble, Sheriff?"

"Not in here, Jenny. I just wanna sit and talk to the man."

"Are you gonna eat?"

"No, I ate."

"I'll bring another coffee mug."

"Thank you."

Jenny left and Bodie looked down at Clint.

"Mind if I sit?"

"I wish you would," Clint said. "I'm getting a cramp in my neck."

Bodie pulled out the chair opposite Clint and sat down.

"Where's that feller, Harvey?"

"He's coolin' off in a cell," Bodie said.

"Thanks for stopping him, so I didn't have to kill him."

"I did it more for him than for you."

"That's okay," Clint said. "I don't care who you did it for. You did it."

Jenny came out at that point, put a mug down on the table. Clint poured the coffee for Bodie.

"Who is he anyway?" Clint went on.

"Just a local," Bodie said.

"What sent him after me with five other men? Or who?"

"I don't know," Bodie said. "When he wakes up, I'll ask him."

"Maybe I should come by the jail and ask him myself," Clint proposed.

"Let me talk to him first," Bodie said.

"Okay," Clint said. "It's your jail."

Jenny came with Clint's breakfast at that point. She set it down in front of him and withdrew. Clint picked up his knife and fork.

"You mind if I eat?" he asked.

"Go ahead."

"What else can I help you with?"

"You can tell me what you're really doin' here in Black Rock."

"I'm trying to find out what went on between Ed Callahan and Tom Angel that made them enemies, made them kill each other."

"Why do you care?"

"Because whatever it was, I got caught up in it, and I killed men I didn't know, and had never met."

"Not the first time you've ever killed someone."

"Maybe not," Clint said, "but when I do it, I like to know why."

"How do you expect to find out?"

"By talking to the people who knew them best," Clint said. "With Angel, I'm guessing that'd be Claire. And with Callahan, his wife."

"When do you intend to go and see Mrs. Callahan?"

"Sometime today, I suppose."

"I'd like to go with you."

"Why?"

"Well, Mr. Callahan was well respected around here. I'd like to make sure his wife is treated with . . . respect."

"I'd certainly treat her with respect," Clint said, "but someone needs to tell her how her husband died."

"Well," Bodie said, "I'm gonna come along . . . if you don't mind."

"And if I do mind?"

Bodie leaned forward and said, "I'm comin' anyway."

Clint shrugged and said, "You're the sheriff."

"Stop by my office when you're ready to leave," the sheriff said, "and don't try to leave without me."

"I'll see you later, Sheriff."

Bodie nodded, took one sip of coffee, then got up and left.

Jenny came walking over.

"Everything okay?" she asked.

"Everything's fine," Clint said. "This food is just great."

TWENTY-SIX

Clint finished his breakfast, and Jenny brought him some more coffee. The place was almost empty now, so she sat down with him.

"What are your plans today?" she asked.

"Talk to Claire, then talk to Mrs. Callahan."

"I'll come with you to talk to Claire."

Why did everybody want to go with him today?

"I think I should talk to her on my own."

"Why?"

"She might say something to me, a stranger, that she wouldn't say in front of you."

"You think she's holding something back?"

"I think if she knew Tom Angel well, then she knows something."

Jenny shook her head.

"I don't know. Claire's pretty . . ."

"Pretty what?"

Jenny shrugged and said, "Innocent."

"Is she?" Clint asked. "I guess I'll find out."

Clint went to Claire's Dress Shop first, found the door

unlocked and Claire inside. She looked up as the little bell tinkled when he opened the door.

"Mr. Adams."

"Claire," he said. "Or should I say Miss—"

"Claire is fine," she said.

She was standing behind the counter. He approached her. She stared at him with wide blue eyes. Clint could see the innocence Jenny was talking about.

"I'm sorry I had to bring you that news last night."

"No, no," she said, "I'm grateful to you. Now I can stop wondering if and when Tom was gonna come back." She shrugged. "He's not. I'll just have to accept that."

"Claire," Clint said, "I need to know what was going on between Ed Callahan and Tom."

"I thought I told you I don't know," she said. "Tom didn't talk to me about his business."

"Was he doing business with Callahan? Was that it?"

"No, I mean—I don't know—I mean, all I meant was, Tom didn't talk much about . . . things."

"So what did you talk about with him?"

"Just . . . things. Not very important things."

"Did you talk about getting married?"

"No, not exactly."

"What do you mean, not exactly?"

"Well, I wanted to," she admitted, "but he never did."

"Claire, I'm finding it really hard to believe that Tom had so much trouble with Callahan and never mentioned it. I mean, the man rode a thousand miles to try to kill him."

Claire played with her long dark hair nervously and said, "I just think you should talk to someone else."

"Is there somebody who knew Tom better than you did?" he asked.

"Not better, exactly," she said, "but maybe in a different way."

"Who was that?"

"His friend Larry."

"Larry what?"

"I don't remem—I think it's Larry . . . Kane? No . . . Cahill, that's it. Larry Cahill."

"Where does he live?"

"Right here in town," she said. "Maybe Tom talked to him about Mr. Callahan."

"Do you know where in town he lives?"

"No."

"What about where he works?"

"One of the stores, I think. I don't know where."

"Do you know Mrs. Callahan?"

"I do, but not well."

"How well?"

"Just by fitting her for dresses when she comes in," Claire said. "She's very beautiful."

"Do you think that might have been the problem?"

"What do you mean?"

"Well, could Tom have been doing . . . something with Mrs. Callahan? And maybe that's why Mr. Callahan wanted to kill him?"

"I don't think so," she said, but she didn't sound real sure to him. That was going to be the first question he asked Larry Cahill when he found him.

"Well, okay, Claire," Clint said. "Thanks for talking to me."

"Mr. Adams . . . you're not gonna cause trouble, are you?"

"That's not my intention, Claire," he said, realizing that wasn't really an answer. "You take care."

"Yes, sir, I will."

He stepped outside and looked around. If Cahill worked in a store, he had a lot to choose from. Clint thought he better get started.

TWENTY-SEVEN

Clint checked a couple of stores and came up empty. He decided this was going to take too long. It probably made sense to ask the sheriff, but he didn't really trust the man. That left him with two other choices—Jenny, and the bartender at the Lucky Eight, Willie. He decided to try Willie first.

As Clint entered the Lucky Eight, he looked around at the few customers who were there drinking. They looked up from their beer or whiskey and, when they didn't know him, went back to their drinks.

The bartender knew him, though, and shifted uncomfortably as Clint approached the bar.

"I'll have a beer, Willie," Clint said.

"Comin' up, Mr. Adams."

Clint waited while Willie drew the beer and set it down in front of him with a hand that shook slightly.

"Nervous about something?" Clint asked him.

"Just—n-no, not really."

"You know a man named Harvey Tracy?"

"Um, I do, yeah." Obviously, Willie remembered that Clint had seen him talking to Harvey at the end of the bar.

"Do you know where he works?"

"I do, yeah."

"Where?"

"Um, he works out at the Callahan ranch."

That was interesting.

"Now I'm going to ask you about another man."

"More questions?" Willie asked miserably.

"Just one, then we're done."

"Yeah, okay."

"I'm looking for a man named Larry Cahill."

"Cahill?"

"That's right. Know him?"

Willie bit the inside of his cheek while he considered the question.

"I'll be very grateful for the answer," Clint said. "And I'll be very disappointed if I don't get an answer. Very disappointed."

"Okay, yeah," Willie said, "I know where he works."

"Good," Clint said. "Where?"

Clint found the feed and grain store with no problem. It was a three-story building at the end of Main Street, across from the livery stable.

He entered and a man wearing a long apron turned and stared at him. He had curly, steel gray hair and a face that looked as if it had been chiseled out of granite. He could have been fifty or eighty.

"Help ya?"

"I'm looking for Larry Cahill. I was told he works here."

"If ya call what he does working," the man grumbled.

"Is he here?"

"Yeah, he's in the back," the man said. "You gonna keep him long?"

"I just need to ask him a few questions."

"You law?"

"No."

"Bounty hunter. You gonna take him in?"

"No both times," Clint said. "I just need to ask him a few questions."

"Yeah, okay," the man said. "Go on back. If you have to wake him up, tell him he's fired."

"Will do. Thanks."

Clint walked to the back of the place, sidestepping bags of feed and grain that were piled almost ten feet high, and found a door to the back. There he found a young man using a shovel to fill some more bags. He was tall, thin, and covered with a thin layer of grain powder.

"Larry Cahill?"

He stopped shoveling abruptly and looked at Clint with a frown.

"Who wants ta know?"

"I do," Clint said. "My name's Clint Adams."

Cahill held the shovel in front of him, as if he'd be able to ward off bullets with it.

"The Gunsmith?"

"That's right."

"Jeez," he said. "Whataya want with me?"

"I just want to ask you a few questions."

"About what?"

"A friend of yours."

Cahill's frown deepened. "Who?"

"Tom Angel."

Cahill lowered the shovel, but maintained his hold on it.

"He's dead," he said. "I heard he's dead."

"I know," Clint said. "I'm the one who came to town with the news."

Cahill thought a moment, then his face brightened and he said, "Oh, okay." Finally, he set the shovel aside. Slapped his hands together to get rid of some dust. "What d'ya wanna know?"

"Well, the main thing," Clint said, "is why did Big Ed Callahan want to kill him so badly?"

Cahill shrugged and said, "I dunno," so quickly that Clint believed him.

"You were friends and you don't know?"

Cahill shrugged again. "He didn't talk to me about that."

"What about Mrs. Callahan?"

"What about her?"

"Could Tom have been involved with her?"

"Maybe," Cahill said. "Tom liked women, and Angela Callahan is a lot of woman."

"But you don't know for sure."

"No, I don't."

"What about his relationship with Claire?"

"What about it?"

"She wanted to marry him," Clint said. "Did he want to marry her?"

"Tom didn't wanna marry nobody. He liked women too much to limit hisself to one."

"I see."

"You need ta know anythin' else?" the young man said, picking up the shovel. "I got work to do, or Old Man Jenkins will fire me."

"No," Clint said, "that's all, thanks."

Cahill bent down to resume shoveling, then turned back and said, "Hey, I got a question."

"Go ahead and ask."

Cahill leaned on the shovel.

"Why'd you get yerself involved with Tom?"

Now it was Clint's turn to shrug.

"He needed help."

"Did he ask for it?"

"No," Clint said, "I just saw him in a bad situation, and stepped in."

Cahill thought a moment, then said, "Huh," and went back to work.

Clint went back out into the main section of the building.

"Was he asleep?" Old Man Jenkins asked.

"No, he was working."

"What a shock. He's probably asleep now, though."

"Well, he was working when I left him."

"Hmm," Jenkins said.

Clint left.

TWENTY-EIGHT

Clint went to the livery, saddled Eclipse, and then walked him to the sheriff's office. He entered and found Bodie was seated behind his desk.

"I'm ready," Clint said.

"For what?"

"I'm going to ride out to the Callahan ranch to talk to Mrs. Callahan."

"I guess nothing's happened today to change your mind," the big man said.

"Nope."

He sighed and stood up.

"All right. I'll get my horse and meet you out in front of your hotel."

"I have my horse already," Clint said, "but I'll walk you over to the livery to get yours."

As they stepped out of the office Bodie, asked, "Who else have you spoken to today?"

"I had conversations with Claire and Larry Cahill."

"Cahill? Why him?"

"He was friends with Angel."

"Who told you that?"

"Claire."

Bodie frowned.

"You didn't know they were friends?"

"No," Bodie said, "but I didn't know either of them real well."

They got to the livery and Clint waited outside for Bodie to saddle his roan. When the man came out, they mounted up and rode out, Bodie in the lead.

"Have you told Mrs. Callahan her husband is dead?" Clint asked as they rode.

"What makes you ask that?"

"Well, Cahill had already heard about Angel being dead," Clint said. "I figure word got around pretty quick. Maybe it got out to her. I'd hate for her to hear it that way."

"Well . . . yeah, I told her. I felt the same way you did, and I thought she should hear it from somebody she knows."

"I thought you said you didn't know her."

"I said I didn't know her well," Bodie said. "She knows who I am, so I thought that would be better."

"How did she take it?"

"How do you think she took it?" the lawman asked. "I told her that her husband was dead."

They rode in silence the rest of the way.

"There's the ranch," Bodie said.

Clint saw a barn, a bunkhouse, a corral, and a large two-story house.

Bodie led the way to the house. As they dismounted, a man came walking over to them, pulling off a pair of gloves.

"Clint Adams, this is Ray Winston, the foreman of the ranch."

Winston was a good–looking man in his early thirties.

"Mr. Adams," he said.

"I told Adams that I was out here to tell Mrs. Callahan about her husband."

Clint thought the foreman looked confused for a moment, then said, "Oh, yeah, of course. Well, she's inside. Come this way."

Winston led them to the front door and inside.

"Wait here," he said. "I'll see if she's ready."

He went into the house while they waited by the door.

When he was out of sight, Winston used the rear stairway to go upstairs. He found Angela in her bedroom. She was sitting on her bed, fully dressed, staring.

"What are you doin'?" he asked.

"Just sitting and thinking."

"Well, Bodie's here with Adams, and he's already told him he told you about Big Ed."

"He must have had his reasons," she said. "Put them in the living room, Ray, and give them something to drink. I'll be right down."

"What are you gonna tell him?"

"I suppose," she said, "that depends on what questions he asks."

He stared at her, but when she said nothing more, he turned and left.

Angela went to her dressing table and sat down in front of it. She touched up her face, rouging her lips and cheeks, then brushed her hair until it shone to her satisfaction.

She stood up, looked at herself. Her dress was blue, cinched in tight at the waist, showing off her full bosom. She thought about changing into something else, then just shrugged and left the room.

Winston led them into the living room and, as they sat, asked, "Something to drink?"

"Whiskey," Bodie said without hesitation.

"Mr. Adams?" Ray asked. "Whiskey? Brandy?"

"I'll take whiskey, please."

"Sure thing."

Winston poured three glasses, handed them theirs, and kept one for himself.

"How's she doin'?" Bodie asked.

"Okay," Winston said. "She's a strong woman. She's in charge now."

"I guess she'll want to have the body dug up and sent back here, huh?" Clint asked.

"Um, I don't know," Winston replied. "She ain't said nothin' about that."

"Well," Clint said, "maybe she's thinking about it."

"Actually, Mr. Adams," she said from the doorway, "I have been."

TWENTY-NINE

She entered the room, and had the attention of all three men. Clint, seeing her for the first time, understood what Claire meant about her being very beautiful. Her black hair was lustrous and long, and her body was lush. All any man could think when looking at her would be *sex*.

"I'm Angela Callahan," she said, approaching him with her hand out.

"Clint Adams." He shook her hand. It warmed his. And she held his longer than was necessary.

"I understand you brought the news of my husband's death," she said. "I appreciate that. Thank you."

"I thought it was the least I could do," he said.

"Why?" she asked. "Did you kill him?" She looked at Winston. "Ray, be a dear and pour me a brandy."

"Yes, Ang—ma'am," Winston said.

"No," Clint said, "I didn't kill him. That was Tom Angel."

"Ah, yes," she said, "Tom. And I understand he's dead, too?"

"Yes."

"Poor Tom."

"You knew him?"

"I did."

"Do you know why your husband wanted so badly to kill him?"

Winston approached her, handed her a glass of brandy.

"Ray, why don't you take the sheriff out and show him that new colt."

"But I thought—"

"I'll entertain Mr. Adams until you get back," she said. "Why don't you give us about a half an hour?"

"Half an hour?"

"There's a dear."

"Uh, yeah, okay," Winston said, "sure. Come on, Sheriff."

Winston and Bodie put their drinks down and left the room. Angela didn't speak until they had heard the door close.

"That's better, isn't it?" she asked. "Now we can talk."

"We couldn't talk with them here?"

"No," she said, "not freely. Not about this."

She was staring at him, and her eyes seemed to be blazing. He wondered if they were even talking about the same thing.

"How's your drink?" she asked him.

Angela had felt something pass between her and the Gunsmith when they touched hands. Suddenly, she wanted the other two men out of the room. Out of the house. She'd never met a man before who had the sheer magnetism the Gunsmith had. And she knew he was feeling the same thing about her.

Could it have been his reputation? She knew what it was about her. Men had looked at her a certain way her whole life, from the time she was twelve years old. Her breasts had started to develop then, and had continued to grow for years after that. When she was sixteen, she had more of a woman's body than any woman she knew.

Yes, she knew by the way he was looking at her that he felt it. But what was it about him?

What was it about him that was making her so wet that she was sure he could smell it?

Clint was erect.

As soon as Angela Callahan had entered the room, he'd felt himself start to grow hard. Now he was fully erect, and she knew it. He was sure she could smell it on him, just as he could smell her arousal on her.

They were two animals in heat. Was that why she had asked for half an hour?

Outside, Bodie asked, "What colt?"

"There is no colt," Winston said. "She wants to talk to him alone."

"Why?"

"Be damned if I know," Ray Winston said. "I don't like it."

"Should we go back in?"

"No," Winston said. "She said a half an hour, and we better give it to her."

"So what do we do?"

"We wait," Winston said sourly. "We just goddamn wait."

She set her glass down, reached behind her to undo her dress.

"We don't have much time," she said. "Twenty-five minutes or so."

"This is crazy," he said. He set his glass down, removed his gun belt, and set it nearby.

"Why is it crazy?" she asked. "I'm a widow."

"Only just."

She removed her dress, pulling it down over her shoulders and breasts, then tugging it down farther so that it fell to her feet. Her undergarments were silk, and expensive. That didn't matter to her. She tore them getting them off, and then stood in front of him naked.

He had removed his shirt and trousers, and now stood there staring at her, his cock making a tent of his shorts.

Her pendulous breasts held his attention, the nipples distended and impossibly dark against her pale skin. The aureoles were dappled with little bumps.

She had a slim waist, flared hips, and a full dark bush between her legs. She was a woman built for a bed.

He slid his shorts down to his ankles, and then kicked them away. If the two men returned now, what would they do, or say?

Crazy!

THIRTY

They were in a rush, feverishly so.

In the back of their minds the whole time was the possibility that the sheriff and the foreman might come back.

Clint took her breasts in his hands, hefted their weight, then lifted them to his mouth. Her nipples were large, fit into his mouth nicely.

"I'm too big," she said.

"Oh, no," he said, caressing one pear-shaped breast, "they're just fine."

"Yes, well," she said, cradling his head to her chest, "in a few years they won't be."

"In a few years I won't be here," he said. "I'm here now."

Between them his hard cock pressed itself against her hot belly.

"I know," she said, reaching between them, "I can feel you."

She fell to her knees in front of him, rubbed his hard penis over her cheeks, then brought it to her lips. She licked the length of him, then wet the tip a few times before taking him into her mouth.

He cupped her head and moved his hips in unison to her sucking action. Finally, she released him and looked up, her eyes shining.

"We'll have to save this for later," she said, "They'll be back any moment."

"Then we better be quick," he said.

He pulled her to her feet, then lifted her and carried her to the sofa. He set her down on it, spread her legs, and drove himself into her. She gasped, wrapped her legs around him, and held on for dear life . . .

They got dressed quickly and Angela asked, "What did you come out here to say to me?"

"Well," Clint said, strapping on his gun, "I wanted to ask you about your husband."

"What about him?"

"What did he have against Tom Angel that took him a thousand miles just to kill him?"

"My husband didn't tell me about his business."

"So you think it was business?"

"What else could it have been?"

"Well, I don't know," Clint said. "Jealousy maybe?"

"Jealousy?" Angela patted her hair into place. "What was there to be jealous about?"

"Maybe you and Angel."

She shook her head.

"No, not me and Tom," she said. "My husband didn't care that much about me. It was something else between those two."

"And nobody else knows what it was?"

"Not that I know of," she said. "So it seems to me you'll never find out."

"Maybe," Clint said, "but I know one thing for sure."

"What's that?"

"I won't find out anything if I stop asking."

He turned to leave.

"Will you be coming back?" she asked.

Before he could answer, Bodie and Winston came walking in the front door, stopped when they saw Clint in the living room doorway.

"What's goin' on?" Winston asked.

"Nothing," Clint said. "I'm done here."

He walked to the front door, opened it, then turned to look back.

"Sheriff? You coming?"

THIRTY-ONE

As they rode back to town, Bodie asked Clint, "What did you find out?"

"Not much."

"She didn't know nothin'?"

"Or she wasn't saying," Clint said.

"You think she's holdin' somethin' back?"

"I don't see how she could not know what was goin' on with her husband."

"You ever been married?"

"No."

"Well, I have," Bodie said. "Believe me, most wives don't wanna know."

"You still married?"

"Not for a long time."

"Mrs. Callahan said her husband wasn't jealous," Clint said. "You know anything about her and any men from around here?"

"You think she was cheatin' on Big Ed?"

"I'm asking you."

"He woulda killed her."

"Not according to her," Clint said. "She said he didn't care about her."

"That don't matter," Bodie said. "She was his, and if somebody was cheatin' with her, he woulda killed him."

"And would he ride a thousand miles to do it?"

"I think he woulda rode to hell and back."

"What went on in here?" Ray Winston asked.

"Nothing," Angela Callahan said. "We talked." She poured herself a drink.

Winston looked around the room suspiciously.

"Talked about what?"

"Big Ed."

"And what did you tell him?"

"I didn't tell him anything, Ray," she said. "Stop barking at me."

He looked her up and down, still suspicious. There was a smell in the room he knew well, one that he usually smelled in her bedroom.

"If you did somethin' with him—" he started, but Angela cut him off.

"How dare you!" she said. "You don't question me, Ray. Remember, with Big Ed gone, I'm in charge, and you're only the foreman."

"Only?"

"That's right, only," she said. "And if you want to keep your job, you'll show me the proper respect."

"What are you tryin' to pull?" he asked.

"I'm pulling my weight, Ray," she said. "Or rather, I'm pushing my weight around, from now on. Now get out."

"Get out?"

"That's what I said," she repeated. "Get out."

"Angela—"

"We'll talk later," she said. "I have to think."

He stared at her, then turned and slunk from the room. She heard the door slam behind him.

As soon as he left, she poured herself another drink and sat down. Her legs were still shaking. She'd never been with a man who fit her so well sexually as the Gunsmith. He'd shown her that it wasn't all about young men. A man with experience, who knew how to use it, could put a younger man—like Ray Winston—to shame.

She wondered what Clint Adams would find out about Big Ed, and when he'd be coming back.

When Clint and the sheriff got back to town, they rode directly to the livery stable.

They walked their horses in and set to unsaddling the animals themselves.

"Whataya plan to do now?" Bodie asked.

"Not sure," Clint said. "It seems like I've talked to everyone I can talk to, and either nobody has anything to say, or they don't want to say anything."

"Maybe there's nothin' to be said," Bodie offered.

Clint rubbed Eclipse down and said, "I can't accept that. A man doesn't have that kind of hate inside him for no reason—and somebody has to know something about it."

"Why?"

"Because that much hate has to come out somehow," Clint said. "There's got to be somebody he'd talk to." Clint had talked to Larry Cahill, Tom Angel's best friend, but what about Big Ed?

"Did Callahan have any friends?"

"Why, sure," Bodie said, "most men have friends, don't they?"

"Who were they? Other ranchers?"

"I don't know," Bodie said.

"Well," Clint said, "maybe that's something I should find out."

THIRTY-TWO

There was a private club in town. In cattle country it would have been known as a Cattlemen's Club. In Black Rock, it was called the Gentlemen's Club.

Clint had nobody in town to confide in, except maybe for Jenny. He went to her café for supper. The place was in the midst of their rush, so Clint simply ordered a steak dinner and ate it slowly. Before he was done, the place had emptied out. Jenny came to his table with another pot of coffee and sat with him. It was she who told him about the club.

"Was Callahan a member?" Clint asked.

"I'm sure he was," she said. "I mean, I've seen him going in and out on occasion when I pass by."

"Okay," he said, "so maybe I can find some friends of his in there."

"But how will you get in?"

"Maybe I can get myself invited in."

"How?"

"Do you know any of the other members? I mean, who they are?"

"Well, maybe," she said. "I mean, I could guess."

"Have any of them ever eaten here?"

"Most of the members of that club eat there," she said wryly. "They don't come in here."

"Okay," Clint said, "maybe the sheriff can help me. Maybe he can steer me toward another member, or get me in himself."

"Clint," she said, "if I was you, I wouldn't trust the sheriff too much."

"Don't worry," he said. "I don't."

She frowned, stared across the table at him.

"Are you all right?"

"I'm fine," he said.

"Did you talk to Mrs. Callahan?"

"I did."

"And? Was she able to tell you anything?"

"No," Clint said. "That is, she says she can't."

"But you think she's holding something back."

"She must be. She was married to Callahan. She's got to know something."

"Maybe you should ask her again."

"Maybe."

"Is that all?"

"What?"

"Is that all you and she talked about?"

She was staring at him oddly, and he wondered if she could smell the other woman on him.

"No, that was it."

"Did you see her alone?"

"Why do you ask that?"

"Well, maybe she didn't want to talk in front of anyone," she said. "That is, if anyone else was there."

"Yes," he said, "the sheriff and her foreman were with us."

"So there you go," she said. "She didn't want to talk in front of the foreman."

"You might be right." He pushed his plate away. "That was great, as usual. I better go and talk to the sheriff now."

"Why don't you come back later," she suggested, "and I'll let you walk me home."

That would mean he'd have to take a bath first; otherwise she would smell Angela Callahan on him.

"I'd like to do that," he said, "if I have the time."

"Well . . . all right," she said, looking a little confused. Maybe she thought he'd jump at the chance to walk her home. Under normal circumstances, he would have.

He smiled at her and left.

"You back so soon?" Bodie asked as Clint entered his office.

"Relax, you're not going to have to saddle your horse again." Clint walked up to the man's desk, but did not sit down. "Remember when I said I was going to try to find some friends of Big Ed Callahan's?"

"Yeah, so?"

"Why didn't you tell me about the Gentlemen's Club?" Clint asked.

Bodie frowned and said, "I didn't think of it."

"Why not? Wasn't Callahan a member?"

"He was."

"So then he'd have friends there, right?"

"Maybe not."

"Why not?"

"The club members are all wealthy men who are competing against each other in the business world," Bodie said. "I doubt you can find two of them who like each other."

"Well," Clint said, "I'd like to try. Would you take me over there?"

THIRTY-THREE

Bodie agreed to walk Clint over to the Gentlemen's Club and try to get him inside.

"Just get me in the door," Clint said. "I'll do the talking from there."

"That's fine with me," Bodie said.

He walked Clint to the new, two-story building that looked like a luxurious hotel. Clint followed Bodie up the stairs to the front door, which was guarded by a doorman.

"Sheriff," the man said.

"This is Clint Adams," the sheriff said. "He needs to get inside."

"Now, Sheriff," the doorman said, "you know I can only let members in."

"I know that," Bodie said, "but maybe you can ask somebody? He's got some news about Big Ed Callahan."

"Callahan?" the doorman said. "He's a member."

"Yeah, he is."

The doorman thought it over, then said, "Wait here."

He opened the door and went inside. Clint stepped up to the door and tried it. It was locked.

"I guess we've got to wait here."

The two men stood on either side of the doorway, watching people go by on the street, until the doorman returned. He opened the door, and stuck out his head.

"You can come in," he said.

Bodie started toward the door, but the man put his hand out.

"Not you," he said, jerking his chin toward Clint, "him."

Clint looked at Bodie and said, "Thanks, Sheriff."

He entered the building, and the doorman closed the door in the sheriff's face.

Inside, Clint found himself facing a well-dressed man of about five-six, forty-five years old or so.

"Mr. Adams?" he asked. "Is that right?"

"That's correct."

"The Gunsmith?"

"Right again."

The man put his hand out and said, "A pleasure. Come with me, please."

"Thanks."

He followed the man farther into the building, past a room filled with men who were sitting in leather arm-chairs, sipping drinks and smoking cigars. They went down a hall to a closed door. The man knocked twice, and then opened it.

"Mr. Adams, sir."

"Thank you, Hellman. That's all."

Clint entered, Hellman closing the door from the outside.

"Mr. Adams," the man behind the desk said. "Please, come in and sit down."

The man was tall, extremely well dressed, about forty with black hair slicked back and shiny with gel.

"My name is Andrew Hopper," the man said. "I manage the Gentlemen's Club."

Clint approached and accepted the hand the man offered to him.

"Please, sit," Hopper said. "Can I offer you a drink?"

"No, thank you." But he did sit, followed by Hopper, who stretched behind his desk.

"I understand you invoked the name of one of our members, Big Ed Callahan."

"That's right."

"I heard that Ed is dead."

"He is."

"And you're the one who brought that news to town?"

"I am."

"Then the story I heard is probably true."

"Probably," Clint said. "Either way, he's dead."

"So then, what brings you here mentioning his name?"

"I need to talk to someone who knew him."

"That would be his wife."

"I already did that."

"And it didn't help?"

"Not much. I'd like to talk to a friend of his," Clint said. "I think another man could tell me what I need to know."

Hopper kept staring at him, as if he expected him to say more.

"So I came here," Clint said. "It seems to me Big Ed must have had some friends here."

Hopper stared.

"Or a friend? One?"

"All of our members are gentlemen, Mr. Adams," Hopper said. "But I can't think of any of them who are . . . well, friends."

"There's got to be one."

Hopper shook his head and said, "I don't think you're going to find anyone here who actually liked Big Ed Callahan."

"Not a pleasant man, huh?"

"It's not that," Hopper said. "These men are all competitors."

"Then why do they come here to drink and smoke together?"

"Honestly?" Hopper said. "Mostly just to brag."

"Okay," Clint said, "okay, that'll work."

"What do you mean?"

"Bragging," Clint said. "There must be somebody Big Ed liked to brag to. Who was his favorite target?"

"I see," Hopper said, "you mean his biggest competitor."

"Yes," Clint said, "maybe he told him something I could use."

"Use for what?"

"To find out why the hell Ed Callahan would chase Tom Angel a thousand miles to kill him. Also, I'd like to find out why I had to kill two of Ed's men."

"But . . . you've killed men before, haven't you?" Hopper asked.

"When I kill a man," Clint said, "I want to know why I had to do it."

"Well," Hopper said. "I think I may have the man for you."

THIRTY-FOUR

"His name is Victor Alexander," Hopper said, "and he is *not* a pleasant man. Not at all. You will notice when we go into the main lounge that he will be sitting alone. He always sits alone—except when Mr. Callahan was here. Then they sat together and tried to top one another with their accomplishments."

They were walking back along the hall from Hopper's office to the main lounge. When they reached it, they stopped in the doorway.

Lowering his voice, Hopper said, "I can't guarantee that he will talk to you."

"Leave that to me," Clint said. "Just point him out."

"No," Hopper said, "I believe I should make the introduction. Come with me."

They entered the room and Clint followed the manager to a small table with two chairs next to it. Only one chair was occupied at the moment, by a white-haired man who was smoking a huge cigar and reading a newspaper.

"Excuse me, Mr. Alexander," Hopper said.

The man's head was encased in blue smoke when he

raised it to look at Hopper and Clint. He did not even squint as he peered through the smoke at them.

"What is it?" he asked, his tone clipped and annoyed.

"I have a gentleman here who would like to talk to you," the manager said.

"About what?"

"About Big Ed Callahan."

"Big Ed," Alexander said. "What a ridiculous affectation. What about him?"

"He's dead, sir," Clint said.

"I heard that," Alexander said. "Why do you want to talk to me about him?"

"I'm trying to find someone who knew him well, sir," Clint said. "I'm told that might be you, as you and he were rivals for a long time."

"Rivals?" Alexander asked. "What a ridiculous concept. We were not rivals, we were colleagues and competitors."

"For a long time?" Clint asked.

"For a very long time."

"If I could just have a few moments of your time—" Clint said.

"Who the devil are you, sir?"

"My name is Clint Adams."

Alexander looked at Hopper, as if seeking confirmation, then looked back at Clint.

"The Gunsmith?"

"Yes, sir."

Alexander put his newspaper aside.

"Why didn't you say so?" he demanded. "Sit down, sit down. Hopper?"

"Yes, sir."

"Go away!"

"Yes, sir."

Hopper gave Clint a look that clearly said "good luck" and withdrew.

Clint sat in the second leather armchair, realized why there were so many men seated in them. It was possibly the most comfortable chair he'd ever sat in.

"Would you like a drink?" Alexander asked. "They have excellent port here. Also, I understand, some quite good whiskey—"

Clint noticed what the man was drinking and said, "A glass of port would be fine."

Alexander waved to a waiter, who was wearing a white shirt, a bow tie, and a vest. When the man came over, the older man said, "Two glasses of port, Evan."

"Yes, sir."

Sitting across from Alexander, Clint realized the man was older than he'd appeared at first sight. His skin was almost translucent, and Clint could see the blue veins beneath it. He must have been close to eighty.

"It seems to me Mr. Callahan was a little young to be a longtime competitor of yours, Mr. Alexander. You appear to have some experience on him."

"Say what you mean, Adams," Alexander said. "I'm an old man. You want a cigar?"

"Sure."

Alexander took a cigar case from the inside pocket of his jacket, opened it, and handed Clint a fat, expensive cigar.

"Cubans," the old man said. "They say they are rolled on the thighs of young Cuban girls. Nonsense, of course, but they are excellent."

The older man struck a lucifer and held it out for Clint to ignite his cigar. Before long they were both puffing out clouds of blue smoke.

At that point Evan returned with their drinks, held the

tray out so the two men could take them. He left without
Alexander thanking him.

"All right, then," Alexander said, "now that we have
drinks, and cigars, what's on your mind, young man?"

Clint thought that it had been a long time since anyone
had called him "young man."

THIRTY-FIVE

Clint explained to Victor Alexander how he'd got in between Ed Callahan and Tom Angel, and what the outcome was.

"Seems to me you should have minded your own business," the old man said when he was finished.

"I think you're right," Clint said. "Other than that, is there anything you can tell me about Callahan?"

"Like what?"

"Like why he might have hated Tom Angel enough to chase him a thousand miles?"

Alexander thought a moment, puffing furiously on his Cuban.

"I didn't know Angel," he said, "so I can't comment on him. And I don't know why Callahan hated him. But I can tell you this."

"I'm listening."

"Callahan hated hard," Alexander said. "If you got on his wrong side in business, he'd crush you."

"Did that happen to you?"

The old man made a rude noise with his mouth and

said, "Of course not. Oh, not because he didn't try. It's just that I'm not somebody who crushes easily."

Clint could believe that of the old man.

"So if he hated a man enough, you could see him chasing him a thousand miles to kill him?"

"Oh, yes," Alexander said, "which is one reason why he would never best me in business. He let his emotions rule his decisions. You see, while he's out chasing that man, his business empire is going to hell."

"What about his wife?"

"Lovely woman," Alexander said, "but that further makes my point. Callahan was foolish to marry a young woman of such obvious beauty and sexuality."

It seemed odd to Clint to hear this old man talking about a woman's sexuality.

"There was no chance he'd ever be able to satisfy her, so the consequences were a foregone conclusion."

"That she would stray, you mean?"

"Yes," Alexander said, "that she would cheat."

"And won't she be in charge of his business interests now?"

"I would hope," Alexander said, "that Callahan made provisions for his businesses in his will. It would be the most foolish decision of his life to put her in charge after his death."

"Wouldn't that allow you to swoop in and take over?"

Alexander puffed on his cigar again.

"What makes you think I want to swoop in?"

"Well, I just assumed, since you were his . . . competitor." He'd almost said "rival" again.

"Competitors, yes," Alexander said, "but not enemies. I have many, many business interests across the country and the world. Quite enough to keep me busy. Why would I want to take on his?"

"But what if his wife mismanages them even before a will can be read?"

"That would be a shame," Alexander said, "and a distinct possibility."

"What would you do," I asked, "if she came to you for help?"

"I don't know," Alexander said. "I might help her. On the other hand, I might not."

Clint puffed on his own cigar.

"I haven't helped you much, have I?" Alexander asked.

"I'm afraid not," Clint said. "I still don't know why Callahan hated Tom Angel. But I appreciate the time you've given me."

"Nonsense," the old man said. "This is a story I'll be able to tell for a while. I had port and cigars with the Gunsmith."

THIRTY-SIX

Clint left the Gentlemen's Club after thanking the manager, Hopper, for his help. The doorman tipped his hat as he left.

What did he have now? Certainly no answers. Was he just going to have to accept that he'd killed two men and been involved in the deaths of three others and never know the exact reason why?

He decided to go to the Lucky Eight and ponder the question over a beer.

Sheriff Bodie went back to his office from the Gentlemen's Club, sat there awhile wondering what Clint Adams was finding out when the door opened and Ray Winston entered.

"Ray," Bodie said. "What're you doin' here? Mrs. Callahan send you?"

"Naw," Winston said, "I came here on my own."

"What's on your mind?"

"Clint Adams," Winston said, sitting down. "We have to get rid of him."

"Why? Does Mrs. Callahan like him?"

"This is not funny, Bodie!"

"What harm is he doing?"

"I'm lookin' at it a different way," Winston said. "What kind of damage could he end up doing?"

"He's just askin' questions," Bodie said. "And he's not getting any answers. At least, he's not gettin' the answers he wants."

"Well, that could change," Winston said. "You've got to get rid of him."

"Sending Harvey and his friends after him didn't work."

"Then maybe you need to send somebody who's a little more experienced. And talented."

"Are you gonna pay?" Bodie asked.

"Don't worry about payin'," Winston said. "I can get Mrs. Callahan to do that."

"Are you sure?"

Even though he wasn't sure about anything anymore when it came to Angela Callahan, Winston said, "Yeah, I'm sure."

"Okay, then," Bodie said, "I know a couple of guys."

"Get more than a couple."

"Well," Bodie said, "as I said, I know a couple of guys, and they know a couple more."

"Then do it," Winston said, standing up. "Do it, Bodie."

"Are you sure this is what Mrs. Callahan wants?" the lawman asked.

On his way to the door Winston called back over his shoulder, "I'm positive."

Outside, Ray Winston stopped and looked around. He knew he had overstepped his bounds, but he felt sure that something was going on between Angela and the Gunsmith, so he needed the Gunsmith out of the way.

For good.

And he wasn't sure he could trust Bodie to get the job done.

But he knew somebody who would.

Bodie sat back in his chair and wondered if this was Winston's idea, or actually Angela Callahan's idea. Maybe he should ride out to the ranch and check, but how could he do that without Winston finding out?

Did he really want to get involved in some kind of plot to kill the Gunsmith? The truth of the matter was, he kind of liked the man.

.

THIRTY-SEVEN

Clint decided to see if he could still walk Jenny home.
When he got there, the door was locked, but when he
knocked, she opened the door.

"I thought I missed you," he said.

"Would it be too forward of me to say that I waited for
you?" she asked.

"No," he said, "it would be flattering."

"Just let me lock up," she said.

He waited while she went back inside, did what she had
to do, then came out and locked the door.

"Shall we?" she asked.

He extended his arm, and she slipped hers through
it. He didn't know what would happen when they reached
her home, but he was still worried that he might smell
like Angela Callahan. However, Jenny had seemed
disappointed earlier when he hadn't jumped at the opportunity to walk her home, and he wanted to make
amends.

"Is it far?" he asked.

"Not far at all," she said.

* * *

They walked a bit, strolled actually, acknowledging the nods and hellos of others.

"Why is everybody so friendly in this town?" he asked.

"There was a time when things were not as friendly around here," she said. "Then Henry Madison became mayor, and he decided that, in order to grow, Black Rock had to have a change of attitude. So he hired Bodie, and most of the undesirables were driven out of town."

"By Bodie? I mean, he's big an' strong looking, but from what I've been seeing, he's not exactly effective."

"Oh, he's very effective," Jenny said, "by appearing not to be."

"So because of his manner—being sort of quiet and unassuming as he is—it's easy for people to underestimate him?"

"Exactly."

"Does he have deputies?"

"He did," she said, "when he was cleaning up the town. But not now."

Clint was concerned. Apparently, he had also misjudged the lawman.

"He had me fooled, too," he said.

"Is that unusual?" she asked.

"Yes," Clint said.

"You're upset."

"A little, yeah."

"I know just what you need," she said.

"A bath?" he asked moments later.

They reached Jenny's small house, which surprised Clint when he got inside. Although from the outside it seemed rather old, the inside had been modernized. She had running water, with a working sink and toilet facility—including a bathtub.

"Yes," she said, "you need a warm bath to relax you."

Also to get the remnants of Angela Callahan off his body.

"You might be right," he said.

"Why don't you sit in the living room," she suggested, "and I'll call you when your bath is ready."

"Okay," he said. "You're the boss."

"Yes," she said, "in my house, I am."

And as if to dispel any chance that he might misunderstand her intentions, she moved closer to him and kissed him.

THIRTY-EIGHT

Ray Winston decided not to wait for Sheriff Bodie to act. In fact, he wasn't even sure the man would act. So he decided to make a move himself.

Everybody in town might have believed that Sheriff Bodie had cleaned out the town, but in truth he had simply created a red light situation. It wasn't a big section of town, but if you knew where to look, you could find someone to take on any type of job.

Winston entered the Black Ace Saloon and walked directly to the bar. He had to walk like he belonged, in order to avoid drawing the attention of everyone in the place. As it was, several men looked up and tracked his progress to the bar. But he had been there before, and there was a man standing at the bar who knew him.

"Well, well," Delmond King said, "look who's here. Hello, Mr. Foreman. What brings you slumming?"

"Lookin' for you, Delmond," Winston said.

"That a fact?" King asked. "Guess that means you're prepared to buy me a beer."

"As many as you want," Winston said.

King turned around and shouted, "Barkeep!"

"Ready!" Jenny shouted.

Clint left the living room, walked down the hall in the direction of Jenny's voice, and then entered the room with the tub.

"It's warm, not hot," she told him.

"That's fine," he said. "I don't really like baths that have steam coming up from them."

"Well," she said, "get undressed and I'll go and get you some towels."

She left the room, and he removed his gun belt and his clothes and slipped into the tub. She was right, it wasn't hot, but it was better than lukewarm. He set his gun down within easy reach.

He looked around and realized he had no soap. He wondered if he was going to have to get out of the tub to find some. At that moment she came back into the room, carrying towels. She had also gotten undressed and was now wearing only a shirt that came down to her hips, leaving her thighs and legs bare.

"I didn't want to get my clothes wet," she said.

"Wet?"

She put the towels down and then held up a bar of soap.

"I'm going to wash your back."

Clint submerged himself to the neck, hoping that the water was getting the last of Angela Callahan off his skin.

"Come on," she said, "lean forward. Don't be shy."

It was funny to him that she was taking his attitude as one of shyness. He sat up, and then shifted forward. She put her hands in the water, lathered them up with soap, and then rubbed them over his back.

"I'm just going to use my hands instead of a cloth," she told him. "I hope that's all right."

"It's fine," he said.

She rubbed his back vigorously, including his neck and shoulders, then began to scratch his back pleasantly with her nails. Clint couldn't help himself, and began to grow hard.

She pushed her hands down into the water to do his lower back, and slid her finger along the crack of his butt. He wondered if it was an accident until she did it again, then slid her hands down to cup his buttocks as he leaned forward even more.

"Mmm," she said, "you have a wonderful bum."

"Thank you."

"Why don't I wash the front of you, too?" she asked.

"Sure," he said, "why don't you?"

When they had two beers in front of them, King asked Winston, "What's on your mind?"

"I suppose you've heard that the Gunsmith is in town," Winston said.

"I heard," he said. "I also heard Harvey went after him. That wasn't a good idea."

"I guess not."

"I wonder who sent him."

"I don't know," Winston said, "but I want you to go after him."

"Alone?"

"I don't care," Winston said.

"You want him dead or just out of town?"

"Again, I don't care," he said. "Do whatever you want."

"And who's footin' the bill on this?"

"Mrs. Callahan," Winston said.

"Why?"

"Adams was involved in killin' her husband," Winston said. "He didn't pull the trigger, but he was there."

"And she blames him?"

"Yes," he lied.

"Well, how much are we talkin' about?"

"I guess that'll depend on how many men you're gonna use."

King waved at the bartender and said, "We'll need two more beers to discuss it."

Jenny ran her hands lovingly over Clint's chest, soaping him up. She did his neck, his shoulders again, his arms, his armpits—which he found so incredibly intimate that it just made him harder—and he popped out of the water.

"Oh my," she said, looking down at him. "I was going to do your legs and work my way up to that, but okay. There you are."

"So you planned this, huh?"

"Oh, yes," she said, "I planned this."

She soaped her hands and then took him and stroked him. She washed his penis up and down, then reached into the water to cup his genitals.

"Oh my," she said with his balls in her hand, "big boys."

"You know what?" he said.

"What?"

"I think you should get in here with me."

"Well," she said, "I have to take my shirt off—"

"No you don't."

He grabbed her and pulled her into the tub, splashing water all over.

"Hey!" she shouted.

He gathered her into his arms and kissed her soundly. She kissed him back, pressing herself against him, but then pulled away.

"Wait, wait," she said. She unbuttoned the wet shirt and peeled it off herself, tossing it out of the tub. Then she put her hands out and posed.

Her breasts were medium sized, and firm, which was surprising for a woman in her thirties. Usually, with woman that age, there was some sag, which he didn't mind at all. He liked breasts of all sized and shapes. Jenny's were exquisite, with small pink nipples.

"You're beautiful," he said. "Now give me the soap."

THIRTY-NINE

In the Black Ace, Ray Winston and Delmond King came to terms on the amount of money that would be paid. Now all Winston had to do was figure out a way to get it. Maybe when Adams was dead, Angela would come to her senses and be his again. With her husband's money, they could live a very comfortable life together.

At least, that was the plan.

Clint soaped Jenny's breasts and then rinsed them off. When that was done, he leaned forward and took the nipples into his mouth. She caressed his head, held him there with her eyes closed. She felt as if she were floating on air.

She reached between them again to take hold of his penis and stroke it. He reached between her legs to touch her, and she gasped.

"Are you ready to get out of the tub and move this to another room?" he asked.

"I am very ready," she said into his ear.

* * *

Sheriff Bodie had made his decision. He was going to ride out to the Callahan ranch and ask Angela Callahan if she'd told Ray Winston to have Clint Adams killed. There was no way he was going to act on Ray Winston's word alone.

In fact, there was no guarantee he would act on Angela Callahan's word either.

"I want it done tonight," Winston said. "Tomorrow mornin' at the latest."

"It'll have to be tomorrow," King said. "My men are in the arms of whores at the moment, and probably drunk. It'll take that long to get them ready."

"Okay," Winston said, "but get it done."

"What about the money?"

"You'll get paid," Winston said, "after."

"I'm gonna trust you, Ray," King said, "because you know what'll happen if you don't pay."

"I know," Winston said.

"Okay, then," King said. "A last beer to seal the deal."

Clint and Jenny dried each other—only right, since they'd washed each other—and then she took his hand and led him to her bedroom. There they fell onto the bed together and became entwined while they kissed—legs, arms, tongues.

"Mmm," she said as his hands roamed over her body, "this is what that first look between us was all about."

"What else could it have been?" he asked, remembering the first look that had passed between him and Angela Callahan. But that was different. That was pure lust. This woman he actually liked.

He rolled her onto her back and began to explore her with all his senses. She felt amazing, smelled sweet, and tasted delicious. She sighed as his tongue moved around her belly button, and then moved farther south.

Finally, he settled between her legs, pushing them apart and then parting the pink lips of her pussy, which was very slick and wet. He ran a fingertip up and down the wet slit and she gasped. Then he leaned in and licked it up and down, causing her to moan and squirm.

"Don't stop," she gasped.

"I don't have any intention of stopping."

And he didn't . . . not for a long time.

Bodie made it out to the Callahan ranch before darkness could fall completely. Several of the men were leaning on the corral smoking and talking, and one came over to him.

"What can we do for you, Sheriff?"

"Is Winston around?"

"Naw, he went into town."

"What about the lady of the house?"

"Mrs. Callahan is in the house, best I know," the man said.

"Okay, thanks."

"Take care of your horse for ya?"

"That's okay," Bodie said. "I'll tie him off in front of the house. I won't be staying long."

"Suit yerself."

The man returned to his friends at the corral, while Bodie walked his horse to the front of the house and tied him off. He walked up the steps and knocked on the front door.

The door was opened by Angela Callahan, who looked surprised.

"Sheriff."

"We need to talk, ma'am."

"About what?"

"Your foreman."

"What's he done?"

"Can I come inside and talk?"

She hesitated, then stepped aside and allowed him to enter.

FORTY

Clint continued to lick Jenny until she screamed and closed her thighs around him.

"Oh my God!" she gasped. "I could have a heart attack if you do that again." She looked down at him. "Do that again."

"Later," he said, gliding up onto her. "First I want to do this." He slid his cock into her easily, since she was so wet. She gasped, and this time closed her legs around his waist.

He slid his hands beneath her, gripped her butt, and began fucking her as if his life depended on it . . .

"He what?"

"Told me you wanted the Gunsmith killed," Bodie said.

"I do not!" she said. "I never told him any such thing. That fool!"

"Relax," Bodie said, "I'm not gonna do it."

"And he'll know that, once he thinks about it."

"So you think he'll do it?"

"No, he won't do it himself," she said. "He doesn't have the nerve."

"He'll get somebody to do it for him," Bodie said. "But he'll have to pay them."

"He didn't have to pay Harvey," she reminded him.

"He won't want another Harvey," Bodie said. "He'll want to hire a pro."

"And that'll take him 'til at least tomorrow," she said. "Won't it?"

"Probably," Bodie said.

"Do you have any idea who he'd go to?"

"No," Bodie said, "but I have an idea where."

"Then you go and find him, and stop him."

"And if I can't?"

"I'll talk to him when he comes back. If not, I'll come to town in the morning," she said. "Between us, we'll stop him, the idiot."

"Mrs. Callahan," Bodie said, "can you tell me why your husband chased Tom Angel until they were both dead?"

They were seated in the living room, on the sofa. She had her hands in her lap, and she stared down at them.

"I think I might be able to, Sheriff," she said. "I think I might."

Ray Winston left the Black Ace, almost satisfied that he'd done what he could to get rid of Clint Adams. There was still one other thing he could do, but he'd have to spend the night in town to do it. Later, he'd explain it all to Angela. She'd see and understand that he had done the right thing.

He walked back toward town.

Bodie left the ranch and rode back to town. Looked like he was going to have to do his job, which he hadn't exactly been doing lately.

*   *   *

Clint rolled over, looked at Jenny's sleeping form next to him. She was exhausted and he was close to being exhausted, but he wanted to clean up so she wouldn't have to do it when she woke up.

He went back to the bath and used the towels to clean up all the water they'd spilled. Then he emptied the tub and cleaned it out. By the time he was done, he was ready for a good night's sleep, even though it was still pretty early.

He awoke to the smell of coffee and bacon. He sat up, rubbed his face, then pulled on his trousers. He left his holster, but tucked his gun into his belt before going to the kitchen.

She turned as he entered, and her eyes immediately fell on the gun.

"I suppose you have to take that with you everywhere?" she asked.

"Yes."

She turned back to the stove.

"Sit down. Have some coffee. Breakfast will be ready in a moment."

"What about your café?" he asked, sitting and pouring himself some coffee.

"It's probably open by now." She turned and came to the table with two plates of eggs and bacon.

"Sorry," she said, sitting opposite him, "no biscuits. Didn't have time."

"This is great."

He forked some into his mouth, nodded his approval.

"So let me get this straight. You can cook like this but you don't cook in the café?"

"Breakfast is one thing," she said, "but I've got a cook who can do anything."

"What's his name?"

"Elroy."

"Does he ever come out of the kitchen?"

"Only to go home. And he goes out the back door."

"I ate in another place when I got here. They told me I didn't want to see the cook. The food was pretty good."

"That'd be Lowell, Elroy's brother. They're not much to look at, but they can really cook."

He put some more bacon and eggs into his mouth and said, "Well, this is really cooking, too."

She smiled.

"Your head is still in the clouds after last night."

"You might be right."

"You wore me out, you know."

"You look pretty well rested to me."

"Well," she said, "I have to go to work, or I'd show you."

"I sort of have some things to do myself."

"Like what?"

"Still asking questions."

"What if somebody decides they don't want you asking questions anymore?"

"Then they'll try to kill me, I guess," he said. "That's probably the way I'll get my answers."

FORTY-ONE

Bodie couldn't find Clint Adams, and he couldn't find Ray Winston.

Adams wasn't at his hotel, and the desk clerk didn't know where he was. It was too early to find him at a saloon. His only other chance was at Jenny's Café.

He didn't know where to look for Winston, so he was just going to keep his eyes open.

Delmond King sat in the Black Ace, which was technically closed to the public. But that didn't matter to him. The bartender was his cousin.

Standing at the bar were his men, five of them. Oh, he knew that Harvey had about the same number of men with him when he went after the Gunsmith, but they weren't pros. These five were. Men who lived by the gun, and wouldn't mind if they died by it. None of them wanted to get old and die in bed.

King looked at the clock on the wall, then looked at the five men.

"It's time," he said.

                    *   *   *

Angela Callahan saddled her own horse in the barn and
walked it out. Ray Winston had not come back from town
the night before, so she was going to have to go there to
fire him.

"You want any of us to come with you, ma'am?" one
of her ranch hands asked.

"No," she said, "I want you all to go to work. I'll be
back soon."

"And Ray?" he asked.

"Ray's getting fired," Angela said.

"Who's the new foreman gonna be?"

"I'm not sure," she said, thinking of Clint Adams, "but
I'm hoping."

She mounted up and rode toward Black Rock.

Clint and Jenny left her house together, started walking
toward town.

"Who else is there to talk to?" she asked.

"I don't know," he said. "Maybe I've talked to everybody I need to. Maybe now I just need to wait and see what
happens."

"Is it really so important to you?" she asked. "The
answer?"

"If there is an answer," he said, "it's important."

"And if there isn't?"

"Then I'll have to accept that, I guess."

They walked together as far as her café. The front door
was open and there were already men seated inside.

"I have to get their orders," she said. "Elroy won't come
out of the kitchen."

"So he'd just leave them sitting there?"

"Yes," she said, "until I come in."

"And they'll wait?"

She looked at him and smiled.

"You've had the food," she said. "Would you wait?"

"Oh, I'd wait."

She put her hand on his left arm.

"Please, be careful."

"I will be," he said. "It's my nature."

"Somehow, I don't think that's quite true," she told him.

FORTY-TWO

Clint went back to his hotel.

He was about to go to his room when the desk clerk beckoned him over.

"What is it?" he asked.

"I thought you would like to know," the young man said, "the sheriff was here early looking for you."

"Thanks for the warning."

"That was not a warning," the man said. "This is a warning. There were six other men here looking for you."

"Six?"

"That's right."

"Led by that fella, Harvey?"

"No," he said, "these were six fellas who look like they know how to use their guns."

"And who was the leader?"

"He stayed outside. I don't know who he is. Sorry."

"That's okay," Clint said. "Thanks."

"Yes, sir," he said. "We try to help our guests."

And keep them alive until they can pay, Clint thought as he went up the stairs.

* * *

Bodie walked into the café, which was busy, as usual.

"Hey, Sheriff," Jenny said. "I think I've got a table for you."

"Not lookin' for a table, Jenny," he said. "I'm lookin' for Clint Adams. Do you know where he is?"

"As far as I know, his hotel."

"No, I checked there earlier."

"Well, then, you missed him," she said. "He just went over there a little while ago."

"Just went?"

She blushed a little as she said, "He didn't spend the night in his room."

"Oh . . . oh!"

"Yeah."

"Uh, okay," the lawman said. "I'll go and check again, then."

"Back to the hotel," Delmond King told his men.

"We checked there already," one of them pointed out.

"Well," King said, "we haven't seen him anywhere else in town, so he's got to show up there eventually. We'll go back there and wait."

"Yer the boss."

Bodie went back to Clint's hotel and stopped at the front desk.

"Did he come back?"

"A few minutes ago," the clerk said. "He's upstairs."

"Did you tell him I was lookin' for him?"

"I did," the clerk said. "I also told him about the other men."

"What other men?"

"The ones that came after you, asking about him," the clerk said.

"How many?"

"About six."

"Was Harvey one of them?" He had let Harvey out of his cell the night before.

"No, not Harvey," the clerk said.

"Did you recognize any of them?" Bodie asked.

"No," the clerk said, "but I think they came from . . . that end of town."

"Ah . . ." Bodie said. "Okay, thanks."

He went up the stairs.

Delmond King and his men stopped across the street from the hotel.

"We'll wait here," he said. "Spread out so we're not so obvious."

"Spread out how far?" one of them asked.

"I don't want us to look like a mob," King said. "Just put some distance between each other. Watch the door, and watch me."

"You know what the Gunsmith looks like?" one of them asked.

"I know," King said. "I seen him once in Abilene. I'll know him."

That satisfied the men, and they began to spread out.

There was a knock on Clint's door as he was strapping his gun back on. He opened the door, saw the big man standing in the hall.

"Sheriff," he said. "What brings you here?"

"I'm here to warn you," Bodie said. "Ray Winston is sending some men after you."

"I know," Clint said. "They're outside my window, trying not to look like a mob."

"You mind . . ."

"Come on in and take a look."

Bodie entered and walked to the window.

"Goddamnit!" he said.

"What is it?"

"That's Delmond King, and some of his bunch."

"Delmond King," Clint said. "I don't know the name."

"Well," Bodie said, "if they kill you, folks will know his name."

"That's a big 'if.'"

Bodie turned to face Clint.

"You ain't goin' out there, are you?"

"Like I have a choice—unless you want to go first. But it's my guess they'd gun you down just as fast."

"You're probably right."

"Tell me, is Winston acting for Mrs. Callahan?"

"She says no."

"You believe her?"

"I do."

"Then it's my guess he's out there someplace, too."

"You're probably right."

"Well," Clint said, "I suppose if I go out there and get gunned down, you can arrest whoever's left. I mean, six to one isn't exactly a fair fight."

"How about six to two?" Bodie offered.

"Not much better," Clint said. "But some."

FORTY-THREE

Clint and Bodie went down to the lobby. The clerk, realizing something was going to happen, got down behind the desk.

"You can go out the back, you know," Bodie suggested.

"Not an option, Sheriff," Clint said. "Not for me. But you can do it."

"No," the lawman said, "I think I better just go out and stand with you. Maybe when they see the badge, one or two of his men will have second thoughts."

"Maybe just enough second thoughts to slow them down," Clint said. "I appreciate this, you know."

"It's my town," Bodie said, "and I've been kinda lazy about doin' my job lately."

"Maybe that's because everybody in town is so nice, huh?" Clint asked. "Sort of makes you think you're not so necessary anymore."

"Maybe," Bodie said, "but I guess this will shake things up some."

"It just might."

"So we just wanna walk out together?"

"And see what happens."

Angela Callahan came riding into town, saw that the street in front of the hotel was suspiciously empty. She was too late. Something was happening, and if she tried to stop it now, she might end up getting shot. She was just going to have to wait for the outcome.

She rode her horse over to a hitching post, dismounted, and tied him off.

"Mrs. Callahan," a voice hissed.

She looked over and saw the young woman who ran the dress show, looking out her door.

"You better come in here and get off the street," Claire said.

Angela nodded, ran over, slipped inside, and said, "Thank you. Do you know what's going on?"

"Not exactly," Claire said, "but it seems like it's gonna be bad."

They closed and locked the door, and then stood at the window together to watch.

"He's comin' out!" Delmond King called out.

"He's got somebody with him!" one of the men yelled.

"Who is it?" someone else asked.

"Damn, it's the sheriff."

"Don't matter," King said. "He's been sheriff too long anyway. Just get ready."

Clint and Bodie stepped out onto the boardwalk and stopped. Clint was surprised the men didn't immediately draw and begin to fire.

"Sheriff!" Delmond King yelled.

"Yeah, Delmond?"

"You sure you wanna be standin' there?"

"You sure you wanna do this with the Gunsmith?" Bodie answered.

"Oh, I'm sure."

"There's somethin' you should know, then."

"What's that?"

"Mrs. Callahan ain't footin' the bill for this."

"What?"

"That's right," Bodie said. "If Winston told you that, he lied to you."

"What's he talkin' about, boss?" one of the men asked.

"Don't matter," King said. "That's the Gunsmith, boys. Come on, let's get famous!"

They all drew . . .

Clint drew his gun cleanly and swiftly, put a bullet right into Delmond King's chest, dead center. Bodie fired, and another man fell from the boardwalk to the dirt.

Clint moved to his left and fell into a crouch as he fired again.

Bodie did the same, stepping to his right . . .

Angela Callahan saw something and ran from the dress shop to her horse.

"Ma'am . . ." Claire shouted, but it did no good.

Angela grabbed her rifle and raced toward the action . . .

Delmond King's men, seeing that he was dead, panicked and began to fire wildly. Facing the Gunsmith had that effect even on professional gunmen.

Clint got to his feet and stepped forward, fired two more times, spinning two men around and dumping them in the street.

Sheriff Bodie stood up, fired one last time to take care of the last man.

The street got quiet.

Clint looked at Bodie, saw that the big man had a crease on his shoulder. There was hardly any blood—yet anyway. He checked himself, saw that he had come out un-scathed.

"They're all down," Bodie said.

"Yeah," Clint said, "but where's Winston?"

From the roof of the building across from the hotel, Ray Winston sighted down the barrel of his gun at Clint Adams. King and his men had failed, but Adams was right out there in the street, as open as he could be.

Winston stood to make sure he could get a good shot, his finger on the trigger . . .

The sound of a rifle shot broke the silence in the street, and both Clint and Bodie looked toward it. Angela Callahan stood there in the street, holding her rifle to her shoulder—and then a body hit the street, having fallen from the roof.

Bodie walked over and took a look.

"Ray Winston," he told Clint.

He stood up and they both looked over at Angela Callahan, who was walking toward them.

"I assume you just saved my life," Clint said to her.

"I'm sorry," she said. "He tried to kill you because of me. And my husband killed Tom Angel because of me. I'm sorry about that, too."

"What do you mean?"

"The sheriff will tell you."

She handed the lawman her rifle, then turned and walked away.

Clint looked at Bodie.

"Lemme get this street cleaned up," Bodie said, "and we'll talk."

They went to Bodie's office and he took a bottle of whiskey from his bottom drawer, poured some into two coffee mugs, and handed Clint one. Then he told Clint what Angela Callahan had told him.

"Let me get this straight," Clint said when the lawman was finished. "She told her husband that Angel had raped her, but he hadn't?"

"Right."

"And that's why he chased him a thousand miles?"

"Right again."

"But he didn't care about her."

"Not as a woman," Bodie said. "Just as his property. Nobody touched Big Ed Callahan's property. But with him out of the way, all his property became hers."

Clint sipped his whiskey and put the mug down on the desk.

"And Winston thought he'd be with her when Big Ed died?"

"That's what she said."

"What if Callahan had come back?"

"I guess they were both hoping Angel would somehow manage to kill him. But I don't know the whole story."

"Maybe we never will," Clint said. "Do you believe her? That she accused Angel of rape? Or maybe they were just lovers, and she lied."

"Whatever happened, Big Ed had one thing in mind when he left here."

"So she's sorry," Clint said, "but she ends up sitting pretty with everything her husband owned."

"Looks like it."

Clint thought about it for a moment.

"Does this satisfy you?" Bodie asked.

"Satisfy? I killed men at the beginning of this, and now I did it again at the end, and for what?"

"Well," Bodie said, "whatever Angela Callahan told her husband, when it comes right down to it, you killed them to stay alive."

"Sheriff," Clint said, pushing his empty mug toward the lawman, "I think that's the way I'm going to have to look at it—and I'll drink to that."

Bodie nodded, and refilled the Gunsmith's mug.

Watch for

TRAIL TO SHASTA

376th novel in the exciting GUNSMITH series
from Jove

Coming in April!

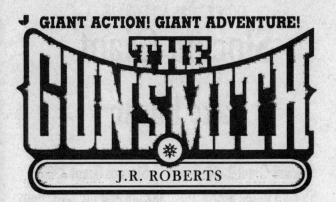

GIANT ACTION! GIANT ADVENTURE!

THE Gunsmith

J.R. ROBERTS

M455AS0812

GIANT-SIZED ADVENTURE FROM
AVENGING ANGEL LONGARM.

BY TABOR EVANS

penguin.com/actionwesterns

M456AS0812

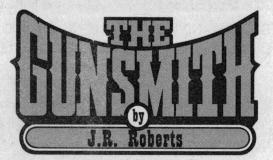